The Wiles of Men

The Wiles of Men

and Other Stories

Salwa Bakr

Translated from the Arabic
by Denys Johnson-Davies

Introductions by Denys Johnson-Davies
and Barbara Harlow

UNIVERSITY OF TEXAS PRESS
AUSTIN

First published in English by Quartet Books Limited 1992
A member of the Namara Group
27/29 Goodge Street, London W1P 1FD

Copyright © 1992 by Salwa Bakr
Translation copyright © 1992 by Denys Johnson-Davies
Introduction by Barbara Harlow copyright © 1993 by
University of Texas Press

First University of Texas Press edition, 1993

⊗ The paper used in this publication meets the minimum require-
ments of American National Standard for Information Sciences—Per-
manence of Paper for Printed Library Materials, ANSI Z39.48-1984.

Library of Congress Cataloging-in-Publication Data

Bakr, Salwá.
    [Short stories. English. Selections]
    The Wiles of men and other stories / Salwá Bakr ; translation by
Denys Johnson-Davies ; introductions by Denys Johnson-Davies
and Barbara Harlow. — 1st University of Texas Press ed.
        p.   cm.
    ISBN 0-292-70800-9 (alk. paper)
    1. Bakr, Salwá—Translation into English.   2. Women—Egypt—
Fiction.   I. Title.
PJ7816.A466A24   1993
892'.736—dc20   93-4648

Contents

Translator's
Introduction

In a writing career that stretches back no more than a few years – her first volume of stories, published at her own expense, appeared as recently as 1986 – Salwa Bakr has established herself at Egypt's most interesting and forthright woman writer of fiction. Two further collections of her short stories, one of which contains the novella *The Shrine of Atia*, came out in the intervening years, while earlier this year her first novel was published under the title *The Golden Chariot That Didn't Take Off Into The Sky*, in which all the characters are inmates of a women's prison.

Salwa Bakr's father was a railways employee and he died before she was born. Having taken degrees in management and drama criticism, she worked for a time as a rationing inspector – yes, Egypt still has rationing of such items as sugar, tea and rice. More recently she travelled to Beirut and Cyprus where she worked as a journalist. She is now married, has a young daughter and lives in an outer suburb of Cairo. It was no doubt due to her political activities as a student that she recently found herself arrested early one morning and obliged to serve a short spell in prison – an experience which she found full of interest and which provided her with the background for her first novel.

The protagonists of Salwa Bakr's stories are in the main working-class women who are struggling in one way or another to provide themselves with the basic necessities of life. Her stories seek to show that the strong are able to exploit the weak by reason of their strength and material advantages, but that the weak themselves only too often contribute to their enslavement through the usually groundless fear that rebelling will only worsen their lot. 'Filching of a Soul', though not one of her outstanding stories, neatly sums up in part the attitude of Salwa Bakr towards the society in which she lives. The inability of the young middle-class couple in the story to resist the social pressure to conform results in their life gradually deteriorating into one of grey drabness. Where working-class persons are concerned the price paid for complacency and passivity is often humiliating servitude and depri-vation. In 'Dotty Noona', the young servant girl with an instinctive yearning for the education she never received is forced to take action when her life, wretched as it is, is threatened with being deprived of the strange form of education that makes up for her drab existence. Salwa Bakr shows that running away can itself be a form of courage. In 'The Wiles of Men', a story with echoes from *A Thousand and One Nights*, the two wives (of the same man) desire nothing more than the security of a roof over their heads. When this is threatened by the prospect of a third wife being introduced into the home, their fears force them to an extreme expedient.

Sometimes in these stories the central character is striv-ing to achieve love, or even just surreptitious sexual fulfilment, or merely a modicum of self-esteem, as in the tragi-comedy of the middle-aged housewife in 'That Beautiful Undiscovered Voice'. The monkey trainer in the story of that title is not being gratuitously cruel, he is merely carrying out the procedure for training monkeys that has been handed down to him. For him the monkeys are not flesh and blood but objects to be moulded to his will and to certain patterns of behaviour that will provide him with a living. It is significant that the trainer meets his match in the one monkey who has the courage to refuse to conform, while his companions live in a mixture of fear and false hope; even more significant is the fact that it is only the monkey who rebels whose condition is bettered. The human condition, Salwa Bakr would maintain, is little different in this respect: politically, economically and socially life has been set in certain moulds and only with courage can one break out of them.

But the price of rebelling against the conventions is sometimes high: the protagonist of 'Thirty-one Beautiful Green Trees', a story in which Salwa Bakr is at her most poignant, merely wishes for herself and others a world that is greener and more colourful than that which most people are prepared to accept. Right from the beginning of the story we are aware of the price she has had to pay for her attempts at improving life since she is writing of her experiences from the confines of a mental home. Several of Salwa Bakr's characters are not only uneducated and under-privileged but are often almost mentally sub-normal, or at least eccentric. It is as though the writer is saying: What is so desirable about being 'normal', when the normal in our society are so often hypocritical, greedy and uncaring.

While containing many of the themes that recur in her short stories, the novella *The Shrine of Atia* is at the same time more ambitious in form. We learn about the central character (a woman considered by many to have been a saint) through statements made by various people who have known her during her lifetime, in answer to an enquiry being conducted by a newspaper. Was Atia really such a saintly character, even though eccentric by the norms of her society? Some of the statements contradict this view and are antagonistic towards her. The people making the statement have their own reasons, their own motives for the views they express, and their statements reveal as much about themselves as they do about Atia.

Salwa Bakr has made her own position clear with regard to feminist literature. In one of the few interviews she has given she expresses the view that women's writing achieves nothing if it is merely directed against men. 'In our backward society,' she says, 'it should play a positive role not only in freeing woman but also the man. What the woman requires in order to realize herself is equally required by the man, for he needs to enjoy the presence of a compatible woman as a life-partner, the presence of a mind that is in tune with his, the presence of emotions that can interact with his own.'

When asked about literary influences, she named Chekhov and Cervantes, both read in translation. These two are unusual choices, as modern Arab writers are more likely to opt for fashionable authors like Camus and Márquez. She was particularly attracted by Cervantes' sense of the ridiculous and his natural though sophisticated methods of story-telling. When talking about possible future projects, she expressed her admiration for Naguib Mahfouz's trilogy and her wish to write a similarly substantial work told from an exclusively feminine viewpoint. Arabic literature, she contends, even more than that of the West, has been the preserve of men and it is the task of women writing in Arabic today to try to redress the balance.

Salwa Bakr is essentially an angry writer. In her opinion, now is not the time – in the political and social context in which she writes – for the telling of stories that merely entertain.

Denys Johnson-Davies

Introduction
Women's Rights, Human Rights

Al-siyasa, "the political," makes only a brief passage through the women's prison in which Salwa Bakr's first novel, *The Golden Chariot Doesn't Ascend to the Heavens* (1991) is set. The political prisoner's categorical appearance there, unnamed as she is, among the more intimately identified "criminals," establishes, however, a critical problematic that underwrites Salwa Bakr's narratives: the status of women's rights as human rights within a collective political struggle.

Aziza the Alexandrian is a prisoner in that same women's prison in Egypt, serving a life sentence for the murder of her mother's husband. Aziza, the novel's main character, assassinated the man, who had seduced her as well as her mother, following her mother's death when, despite his apparent promises to her, Aziza, he took another woman as his new wife. Aziza plans to leave the prison in a golden chariot destined for the heavens, but she does not intend to leave alone. Bakr's novel describes not only Aziza's liberation project, but also the other women prisoners who have been elected to accompany her and the life histories that have warranted them a place in Aziza's chariot.

Um Ragab, for example, became a pickpocket in order to support her children. After forty-five years as a sexual slave and domestic to her husband, Hana killed him one night by leaving on the gas under a cooking pot. Azima, "the Tall," too tall, that is, to get married, and who became a *naddaba* (professional mourner), then a vocal performer at religious celebrations, and finally a popular singer, killed her abusive lover. Aida, from Upper Egypt, is in prison on her brother's account, having taken the blame on her mother's orders for his honor and revenge killing of her battering husband. Huda, at sixteen, mother of two and a drug addict, is the youngest prisoner. Zaynab Mansur, referred to in the company as "madame," is the best-educated and most cultured among the prisoners. The story of Dr. Bahiga Abd al-Haq, in prison for alleged "malpractice," describes the painful difficulties and contradictions of lower class women who have succeeded in entering the professional ranks. Shafiqa had been a beggar. Um al-Khayr, a peasant, is likened to a Pharaonic goddess. Gamalat assaulted her sister's would-be boyfriend. And so on. Twelve prisoners in all are to accompany Aziza in that "golden chariot to the heavens."

The place of the anonymous political prisoner—is she a Muslim or a Communist, Aziza wonders at first—within these narratives then is significant, both for Aziza's project and to Bakr's work. If the "politicals" remain isolated, as Aziza points out, from the "people," Aziza's own liberation project is itself still not consciously constructed as an effective political agenda or a collectively organized movement. The golden chariot remains an escape from, rather than a challenge to, the system in which she and the other women inmates—including the "political—are imprisoned.

Set in prison, Bakr's fictional narrative not only proposes a contemporary sociology of Egyptian women and gender relations through their "oral histories," but argues as well the necessary if conflicted connection between women's issues and their historical, political, institutional, and especially familial contexts. What the state, and with it the traditional order, construes as women's "crimes" punishable by law are recast as gender issues, women's responses to systemic abuses, mediated by class oppression, against the women themselves. Rather than the salvational "golden chariot to the heavens" imagined by Aziza in prison, however, the novel suggests the necessity of emancipatory projects for social and political change grounded in the current historical conditions—both regional and global—and the material realities of women's lives.

Zeinat, heroine of the title story in Salwa Bakr's first collection, *Zeinat at the President's Funeral* (1986), had proceeded differently from Aziza in seeking redress for women's disenfranchisement. A poor woman, she became a writer—of letters to the President of the Republic, in the hope that he would amend her meager pension. Whereas her first petition had been requitted, her second went unheeded, and any attempt actually to approach the head of state, whether in his car or in his coffin, was violently thwarted by his own entourage. But the "bread riots" in which Zeinat would later participate under the regime of that President's successor were the occasion as well for Om Shehta to mobilize on behalf of her own demands. "Om Shehta Triggered Off the Whole Affair," from the same collection, identifies the crucial role played by women in precipitating social and political change, a role acknowledged neither officially nor unofficially. If Om Shehta "triggered the whole affair" by leading the women to the Governorate and the Police Headquarters to protest the removal of food subsidies, it is instead Hussein Diab, student, intellectual, and aspiring activist, who has been detained. In prison however, the man now reflects self-critically: "'Something's wrong' he thought. His thighs shook nervously: 'She should have been here, in my place'" (*Such a Beautiful Voice*, 107).

While arresting Om Shehta might indeed have credited her with political status, incarceration by the state that has deprived its women and its poor of subsistence supports would at the same time only reconfirm its denial of the basic human rights of those dispossessed peoples within its subject citizenry. Om Shehta, like Zeinat before her and Aziza after, and like the other women inhabitants of Salwa Bakr's narratives, is demanding recognition, recognition of her identity as a woman with equal access to the perquisites and privileges of her male counterparts, and an identification of their demands with those of the society at large. As Sherif Hetata, an Egyptian intellectual and political activist who himself spent more than a decade in Egypt's prisons, has argued in his "testimony" on a "changed male opinion on the women's movement in Egypt," the vision of a democratic social order does not, cannot, allow for the separation of the "general" (*al-ʿamm*) and the "particular" (*al-khass*), an ideological separatism that necessarily serves to preserve the interests of existing and unequally distributed power relations premised on distinctions dogmatically drawn along lines of gender, religion/ethnicity, and class. Nor is it simply a rhetorical matter of the now standardized debate between traditionalism and modernization, for the socialist movement, Hetata charges, no less than the conservators of received values, has been historically disinclined to consolidate within its own analyses the practical needs and emancipatory perspectives elaborated by women inside and outside the movement alike. Hetata, who emphasizes the influence on his own social and political rethinking of the ideas and activities of his wife, the distinguished Egyptian feminist Nawal al-Saadawi, maintains not only that women must organize among themselves but that new connections between women and men must be construed and constructed, reorganized, by all prospective parties to progressive change.

The Wiles of Men, this anthology of thirteen stories and a novella taken from Salwa Bakr's first three collections, depicts social and cultural life in today's Egypt, spanning the four decades since that country gained its independence, and under the rule of its first three presidents, Gamal Abdel Nasser, Anwar Sadat, and Hosni Mubarak. That narrative depiction outlines the economic and political changes of those decades that have affected the daily lives of ordinary Egyptian women. From the title story, "The Wiles of Men," which tells of the effort of two co-wives, neither of whom has borne a child, much less a male offspring, to prevent their husband from marrying now still a third, to "A Small White Mouse" and its tale of government harassment of struggling street vendors, Bakr's writings intimately portray the subtle but unrelenting pressures on women from both inside and outside the domestic space. "Thirty-one Beautiful Green Trees" and "That Beautiful Undiscovered Voice" suggest the difficulties that women have in the very telling of their stories—to their society, to each other, or even to themselves. "Dotty Noona," "An Occasion for Happiness," and "The Sorrows of Desdemona" recount too the obstacles to women's education that are thrown in their way by family and system alike. The short novel, *The Shrine of Atia*, relates in turn the kind of stories that get made up by others—neighbors, lovers, sheikhs, children—about women whose lives have, even slightly, deviated from the prescriptions of their conditions.

"Now is not the time," writes Denys Johnson-Davies in the translator's introduction, "in the political and social context in which [Bakr] writes—for the telling of stories that merely entertain." Salwa Bakr's stories may not indeed be simply entertaining but they are compelling in the quiet passion and subtle detail with which they represent the struggle for a day-to-day life waged by Egyptian women despite the odds, small and large, arrayed against them by the contemporary social order. Like Sayyida, who has discovered her own "beautiful voice," and is taken by her husband to a doctor who prescribes tablets to cure her of the discovery, Noona is declared "loony," dotty, for having learned from the recitations in the school building adjacent to the home in which she works as a servant. Mad or criminal, then, these women are concertedly protesting the calculated and systematic exclusion of the urgent issues of women's rights from the purview of concern over human rights.

The "eloquence of struggle" (*balagha al-ghilaba*) is how Ferial Ghazoul has described the writerly strategies of Salwa Bakr's narratives in their contestation of the evacuation of the transitive potential and effective meaning in contemporary Arab discourse. For Ghazoul, Bakr's stories are written from and for the social space of those "deportees," the ones who have been "removed (*mustabʿadun*) from the centers of power and the sites of authority" (108). "Fools," women, and children, like "dotty Noona," argues Ghazoul, have long provided, in speaking out in literature for themselves and others marginalized like themselves—*muhamishun*—the insights into the abuse of power that enable analysis for change. In her reading of the story of Noona, the critic examines the dynamic of cultural contradictions and linguistic struggle that both animates and activates Salwa Bakr's deployment of the transitive potential of language: city and country, rich and poor, male and female, lettered and unlettered. Ghazoul concludes, then, that "Bakr's artistry lies in her use of narrative and colloquial language to open the present to the future. . . . [Bakr] thus seeks to get at the very conditions, aspirations, and modes of subsistence in our traditions and our practices in order in turn to present popular reality and popular symbolism at one and the same time—a brilliant example of the eloquence of struggle" (122).

Those cultural contradictions and the political struggle that they enjoin for the stories' protagonists and readers alike inform women's activity and activism in contemporary Egypt as well. While in *The Golden Chariot Doesn't Ascend to the Heavens* Salwa Bakr chose the novel as the form and prison as the setting for her re-examination of women's location in the gender order and the various ways in which they resist this positioning, her text also mobilizes the political prisoner's silence in combining the generic and disciplinary diversity of personal account, ethnographic report, cultural critique, review essay, and political analysis, collectively suggesting the reciprocal and developing parameters—academic and activist, institutional and popular, official and unofficial—for engaging with women's issues precisely through women's own engagement with these issues. The Women's Health Book Collective in Cairo, for example, produced an important volume, *Hayat al-mar'a wa sihhatuha* (Women's Life and Health), based on *Our Bodies, Ourselves* but radically adapted to the specificity of the concerns of Egyptian women. This book was published in 1991 after more than five years of collaborative preparation. Hind Khattab's *The Silent Endurance* on the social conditions of women's reproductive health in rural Egypt was published in 1992 by UNICEF and the Population Council. At the same time, however, the Arab Women's Solidarity Association (AWSA), founded in Egypt in 1985 by Nawal al-Saadawi, was closed six years later in June 1991 by the Egyptian government. Women in Egypt, that is, are continuing to engage with the social and political exigencies that interrupt their lives. Following an Administrative Court verdict in May 1992 that upheld the decision of the Social Affairs Ministry to shut down the AWSA and turn its assets over to another association called Women in Islam, al-Saadawi argued that the "government wants women to be involved only in charity organisations. But, she added, any issue related to women or to the public in general cannot be separated from politics. 'Everything is political,' she said, 'even if we are asking for water purification, because we will have to ask the government for more funds and this is a political matter'" (*Al-Ahram*, 14 May 1992). Thus too, the fifth issue of *Al-mar'a al-gadida*—or "the new woman"—(1992) was devoted to the question of violence against women. No less importantly, Salwa Bakr herself, together with Hoda el-Sadda, has recently begun the editing and publication of *Hagar*, a journal on women's issues as these are being redefined in literary-critical and socio-political arenas.

In September 1992, by contrast, a Saudi feminist's application for refugee status in Canada was rejected by the Refugee Board, who admonished her that she would "do well to comply with the laws of Saudi Arabia" (see *The ACTivist*, 10 October 1992). The woman's own argument on behalf of her application, however, had insisted that she faced discriminatory political reprisals in that same country for her outspoken opinions on the repressive conditions and legally demeaned status of women. Women's rights, that is, are human rights and must be recognized as such by national administrative apparatuses and international human rights instruments alike. Egyptian women who, unlike Om

Shehta perhaps, attained the distinction of incarceration for their public work, have documented the urgency of the recognition of the social—and political—status of women. Nawal al-Saadawi's *From the Women's Prison* (1982) and *Prison: Two Tears . . . and a Rose* (1985) by Farida al-Naqqash, like Safinaz Kazim's *On Prison and Freedom* (1986), detail, from the variously different perspectives of socialism and Islam, the experience of political detention under Anwar Sadat's infitah regime and Egypt's compromised peace with Israel. Earlier Zaynab al-Ghazali had described imprisonment in Nasser's concentration camps in her memoir, *Days of My Life.* More recently still, Latifa al-Zayyat, novelist, critic, and political activist, has recounted the same period in her autobiography, *Search Campaign: Personal Papers* (1992).

In concert then with the Thirty-seventh Session of the United Nations Commission on the Status of Women (1993), and following the example of the Zeinats, Om Shehtas, Azizas, and Noonas in Salwa Bakr's stories, Egyptian women—writers, researchers, intellectuals, and popular mobilizers—are demanding that women's rights be recognized as human rights. The issues proposed for the UN discussion on women in Vienna in 1993, preparatory to the 1995 meeting in Beijing, include women's legal literacy, conditions of women in extreme poverty, the inclusion of women's concerns in national development planning, and the participation of women in the peace process. These same issues have set the narrative agenda for Salwa Bakr's stories as well.

Aziza the Alexandrian dies in the last chapter of *The Golden Chariot Does Not Ascend to the Heavens*, just as she is making final preparations for the chariot's departure. The chariot, as the novel's title concludes, "does not ascend to the heavens." Aziza's project, however, is even now being given many new organizational shapes and multiple innovative routes, while the skies themselves are being relocated on the ground, in the shifting political, social, and cultural map of the Arab world and the international order.

Barbara Harlow

References

Bakr, Salwa. *Zaynat fi jinaza al-ra'is* (Zeinat at the President's Funeral). Cairo: n.p., 1986. Stories.

———. *Maqam Atiya* (The Shrine of Atia). Cairo: Dar al-Fikr, 1986. Stories.

———. *ʿan al-ruh alati saraqat tadrijiyan* (Filching of a Soul). Cairo: Misriyya, 1989. Stories.

———. *Al-ʿaraba al-dhahabiyya la tasʿad ila-l-sama'* (The Golden Chariot Does Not Ascend to the Heavens). Cairo: Sina, 1991. Novel.

———. *ʿagin al fallaha* (The Peasant's Dough). Cairo: Sina, 1992. Stories.

———. *Wasf al-balbal.* Cairo: Sina, 1993. Novel.

———. *Such a Beautiful Voice.* Translated by Hoda el-Sadda. Cairo: General Egyptian Book Organization, 1992. Stories.

Ghazoul, Ferial. "Bilagha al-ghilaba." In *Al-fikr al-ʿarabi al-muʿasr wa-l-mar'a.* Cairo: Arab Women's Solidarity Association [1992].

Hetata, Sherif. "Shahada: nazra dhukuriyya mutaghayyira li-l-haraka al nisa'iyya fi misr." In *Al-fikr al-ʿarabi al-muʿasr wa-l-mar'a.*

Middle East Report. Special issue on Gender and Politics. 173 (November–December 1991).

1

The Wiles of Men

There was a knock at the front door. The person arriving
was the awaited bridegroom. Faheema the seamstress gave
a gulp of joy and clapped her hand to her breast, then said
to herself, 'How fortunate I am! O how happy I am after
all this waiting and longing!' She hurried off to take a
good look at herself in the mirror to make sure about the
lipstick she'd put on and the *kohl* on her eyes. She also
arranged her hair and what have you, and a mere five
minutes later she had entered the parlour where the bridegroom was sitting with her uncle, with glasses of fruit
juice. The two of them drank and said to her, 'Congratulations, Faheema.'

It wasn't more than a few weeks before the contract
was made out and the marriage consummated. Faheema
was beside herself with joy, not believing it had actually
happened, many times thinking herself to be in a dream.
She went on talking to herself as she dusted and washed,
swept and cooked, saying, 'Glory be to Him who forgets
not His poor servants! By God, everything has turned out
fine, and it has happened to me when I thought it would

never come right. The good God has given me a husband, the very best of men, and his radiant face and my contented life with him are the envy of women; I used to think that nobody would ever look at the likes of me, because of my looks and my shabby clothes, my shortness and blackness, but the blessings of God are ordained, the fates are written. If only time will keep me together with him so that I may be his faithful slave and contented wife. Glory be to Him who has changed me since the consummation of the marriage so that now my bones are covered with flesh and my face is so rounded out and glowing that my over-long nose is set back into it! Here I am looking really feminine, all dressed up in red and green. How right are they who say, "A person is half what he looks like and half what he wears," and, "Dress up a reed and it becomes as pretty as a doll." '

But nothing lasts for ever, and were it to last for someone else it wouldn't find its way to you. Thus the merchant, who was once her bridegroom and had become her beloved husband, was seized with apprehension as the days and months passed by and the year was concluded and Faheema's womb had quickened neither with son nor daughter – he who so wanted to have godfearing children by some good woman previously untouched by man. And this is why he had chosen Faheema, though he knew that amongst women she wasn't thought of as beautiful and wasn't worth a fig in the market of women. But he, a well-informed expert on the subject of women, having had experience of the brown-skinned and the blonde, the long and the short, the fat and the thin, and having tasted from them the pleasures of life, knew that desire was one thing and marriage another. The latter requires someone

2

who is modest and well mannered, decorous and dignified, because, my lad, if you were to marry a flighty and
beautiful woman, she might sleep around and make you
suffer with her charms and her coquetry, and you're a
man who spends all day long in the bazaar and goes back
home only in the evening. Also, you have got to know,
ever since you began wandering about and leaping around
in the world of women on entering the state of manhood,
by reason of your youthful good looks, your standing and
wealth, that all women are the same at night.

But Faheema, my lad, has produced no child, so what
are you waiting for? Why the distress and forbearance?
You'll only burn yourself up and be ruined by drinking
every night through sadness and grief. By God, if the
fault lay with you, I would shut up and resign myself,
and would continue life with the woman as things are,
for this would only be destiny as it has been written and
your lot as it has been ordained. But you know yourself,
you who have lived with a large number of women, and
had it not been for your knowing a doctor who aborts
her who is pregnant with the ease and facility of someone
drinking a glass of water, you would by now have had
not one child but ten. But Faheema has let you down,
you who reckoned she'd be in bloom at the first watering
and would bring you the boy and the girl you want. But
glory be to God, who certainly acted in wisdom, for
though the son of Adam rushes around and about like the
beasts, he'll get no more than what is coming to him!

Then, after he had arranged everything, he got together
with Faheema at a moment when she was in a good mood.
He informed her that he had married a young peasant girl
and would be bringing her to live with them in the spacious house they occupied, that life would continue
between them as before, that nothing in their circum-

stances would be altered and that full power would remain with Faheema, for he found no justification for divorcing her and wished to go on being with her. She should, nevertheless, be careful, extremely careful, not to vex the young girl or pick quarrels with her, for he didn't want a headache every other day, and he didn't want people to see the three of them having disagreements. Then, having wiped away the tears that flowed down her cheeks like rivers, and kissed and fondled her, he presently closed the bedroom window and drew her by the hand to the bed.

As for what the merchant said to his new bride, when bringing her with him from the country to the city for him to consummate the marriage and for her to take up residence in his house, it was really scary. It shook her and brought fear to her heart, for he told her she would have to be obedient and compliant to his first wife, would have to carry out her orders and take her advice in everything and not contradict her or argue with her, especially not in front of other people and the neighbours. He also told her he wouldn't stint her in anything and would improve her circumstances and keep her in happiness and comfort, denying her nothing, so long as she followed his advice and kept to his words as though they were rings in her earlobes. Then, indicating that she should spread out her fingers, he took out of his pocket a gold ring with a large red stone in it and slipped it on one so that the peasant girl went almost mad with a joy that coursed through her limbs the whole of the night, after she had eaten the roast duck and the rice pudding with nuts and raisins, in the room in which she had been wedded to the merchant, whose longing that night for a little girl or boy increased more and more to the point that he was almost crazy, wanting to hear, be it just once in his life, someone calling out 'Father'.

But the passing of the days and the approach of the end of the first year of his new marriage left him extremely surprised at the state of affairs with this young girl, so solidly built and with such vigorous health, who never complained of any weariness or illness, and who ate like a grown man – the rosiness of her cheeks and the sparkle in her eyes were the proof of this – and yet who hadn't got herself pregnant with boy or girl or mentioned any aches or pains that might have prevented it. Thinking it over, he said to himself, 'Perhaps some spell has been cast on me or some trick played against my wife.' The fact is that the first person he suspected was Faheema, for he knew the extent of her love and devotion and also of her jealousy, so he hastened to open the subject with her after first being nice and gentle; Faheema swore, however, that she hadn't been to a sheikh who was in league with any demons, or to a trickster or a sorcerer, despite the fact that she had thought of doing so when he had first spoken to her about the question of his new marriage, for she loved him and hoped he would be hers alone. But when she had seen the peasant girl and got to know her, and realized she was a poor thing who had lost her mother and had suffered at the hands of her step-mother, she became fond of her and treated her like a good and sincere friend, especially as the peasant girl showed her nothing but affection and respect. And so she said to herself, 'And why shouldn't this young girl have a beautiful child whom the three of us could love and who would fill the house with his joyful laughter. And if my co-wife is his mother, and my husband is his father, then, by God, I'll be a second mother to him, I'll sow my love in his heart with my tenderness and affection for him, for motherhood isn't just the womb that carries, nor the breast that gives suck, but affection and protection, compassion and sympathy.'

When the merchant heard these words from his first wife, his weary breast found rest and his mind calmed down in respect of her, and he was seized with pity for Faheema; so he caressed her and reassured her of his fondness for her, then thanked her for her kind thoughts and intentions, and rose to his feet so as to go out to his business in the bazaar.

However, not many months were to pass before Faheema received the news that her husband was considering marrying a third wife. She went quite out of her mind. At first, she refused to believe the news at all, then she clapped her hands together in despair as she said, 'The man's gone absolutely crazy. Is he going to marry yet again when he's over fifty? Does he think the new one's going to give him the child he wants? Doesn't he realize that he's sterile and that there's no hope of his siring children and having offspring?' When night came, she was still brooding and turning things over in her mind from every point of view. Fire flared up in her heart and from God knows where she sniffed out the danger in this new marriage. Apart from anything else, it occurred to her that the house wouldn't be large enough for a third woman to share their life. For days she went on like this, waiting for the merchant to speak to her, as was his wont, while she examined the news that came to her from here and there. When he didn't speak to her and became more loving and tender with her, she felt there was an even bigger danger, and her feelings towards him changed and she began to look at the matter with a different eye.

Faheema said to her co-wife, who was no longer a peasant girl, for she had been altered by the ways of the city and had discarded the black head-covering and kerchief and had put on clothes that were short and tight: 'Suppose our husband were to marry a third wife, what would your opinion be?'

The naïve young girl laughed, having removed the clothes-peg from between her lips and fastened it on her dress which was stretched out on the line, and said, 'And has he still got the strength for a new woman? He has reached a state where he sleeps like the dead. Don't you hear his snoring every night? And haven't you noticed how heavy his footsteps have grown when he walks? But why should you worry yourself about him so much, thinking about something that's not going to happen? Aren't we eating and drinking and living a relaxed life in ease and comfort? Why, then, the anxiety? What more do we need from life?'

Faheema, however, scared her and silenced her with looks, giving her details of the news she had received and explaining to her co-wife the danger of having a new woman to share their life. With the merchant getting on in years he might well divorce them both or at least divorce one of them. At this the heart of the peasant girl shrank in terror, frightened that she would become homeless in the event of being divorced, so she said to her co-wife, 'So what's to be done?'

'If you're straight with me and I'm straight with you,' Faheema replied, 'and we pledge ourselves sincerely and in good faith, and stand together in facing up to things, our ship will be saved and our life will be safeguarded, with you a poor thing, like a branch lopped off a tree, and I in almost the same position, especially as my uncle, my sole remaining relative, has one foot in the grave.

Why shouldn't we be like two sisters, even if we're not from one and the same womb, with me having no one but you, and you having no one but me? Let's get rid of that fatuous man. May God be with us.'

Then there was a knock at the door and the conversation was discontinued since the person arriving turned out to be the merchant, who called out to them to come down from the roof where they had been hanging out the washing.

A week later the merchant sat as usual between his two wives at supper and began to eat the rabbit they had prepared for him. The peasant girl didn't like rabbit and couldn't bear the sight of it because it looked like cat, besides which she was having her period, so she just had the *mulukhiyya* with the rice. As for Faheema, she declined the food, pleading various pains in her gall-bladder. The merchant, however, ate happily of the rabbit, and then drank tea with enjoyment, while Faheema and her co-wife exchanged glances in silence. After his meal the merchant went into the co-wife's bedroom, turned on his back, and went to sleep.

It was soon after the setting of the stars and the first glimmerings of dawn that the merchant began tossing and turning in his bed like an animal twisted in pain, with the two women weeping and wailing alongside him. With the coming of dawn the man's eyes were wandering and he was at death's door. When the peasant girl saw this she began to shriek and bewail the loss of husband and breadwinner, while Faheema wept and lamented on the other side of the bed. Whenever the two of them were about to go off to fetch a doctor or an ambulance, the merchant would vehemently refuse and stop them doing so by saying that in a while he'd be better. When the cock gave its first call – cock-a-doodle-doo – the man's head fell back on to the pillow and his two hands stretched out motionless alongside him. Faheema pounded her chest and sobbed, while the peasant girl started to go out of the house to call the neighbours. While the two of them were thus engaged, the merchant suddenly jumped to his feet, fit and well in the middle of the room, and all the two women could do was fall at his feet in abject terror.

When the two women recovered they found the merchant sitting on the sofa in the living room, as usual of a morning, sipping a glass of tea which he had prepared himself, while listening to the news of the government on the radio. Seeing the two of them coming towards him, he smiled derisively and laughed. Then, ordering them to stand in front of him, he told them he knew all the details of their plot to poison him – the druggist whom they had asked for the poison had given them away, having sold them salt instead of poison. Then he informed them that he had made a pretence of dying in order to frighten them and see what they'd do next. He was now quite persuaded that they were a couple of criminal whores who deserved nothing better than to be flung into prison, or to be dismembered and the pieces thrown to the dogs in the street.

When the two wives heard these words they burst out crying and wailing and grovelled at his feet begging his forgiveness. Faheema kissed the ground between his feet and said that she had done it only because of her passionate love for him. Her co-wife said the same thing. Then Faheema added that with him at the age he was, she was frightened he would fall into the grasp of women. As for the peasant girl, she implored him to kill her or throw her to the dogs but not to divorce her or send her to prison. They went on like this for about an hour with the man enjoying their misery and distress until he got a headache from all the wailing and talking, so he said to them, 'Do you think I'll tell the government? By God, not a bit of it, for I don't want anyone gloating over my misfortunes; also I'm afraid for my reputation and my business from idle gossip. Do you think I'll divorce the two of you? By God, never. After what you've done to me, I'll not let you go. I'll treat you like a couple of dogs, I'll break you and torment you to my heart's content.'

The merchant got up from where he was sitting and dressed himself for going out. Then the two wives, who had been cowering in a corner of the house shivering with fear, heard the slamming of the front door. They stayed like this, without food or drink, not moving from where they were, blaming and accusing each other. They were utterly overcome by remorse and time flew by without their noticing until they heard the creaking of the front door being opened and they got up and went into the living room where the clock hanging on the wall pointed to midnight.

The merchant was standing there; at his side a pregnant woman with protuberant stomach was leaning on his arm. He said to them, 'This is my wife who will, God willing, be the mother of my children. A while back I went through a common law marriage with her.' He looked extremely drunk. He added that he had not intended for her to live with them in that house, but now he had decided, after what they had done the previous day, to bring her to live with them and put her in complete charge. Then he indicated Faheema's room, which was the most spacious in the house, and turned to the pregnant woman, saying, 'This is your room and everything in the

10

house is yours, and I have bequeathed to you all my business and possessions.' Then he turned to the two wives and said, 'I have divorced the two of you irrevocably and without a possibility of remarriage.'

Then his breathing became heavy, his voice more and more quavery, and down he fell, there and then, dead.

2

Thirty-one Beautiful Green Trees

Before telling the story let me say, right at the start, why
it is I decided to write it and set it down precisely as it
happened to me, just as I have lived it and felt it moment
by moment until they brought me to this terrible place.
So isolated am I from the world that I have become wholly
convinced there is no hope of ever being released, unless
it be to go to the world of the dead. Thus it was that I
said to myself: Write it, my girl. Kareema Fahmi, write
your story in detail and hide it away in some safe place,
perhaps in the mattress, having scooped out a little hole
in one of its sides, so that maybe one day someone will
find the pages you've written and will feel pity for you,
realizing how wretched you were when, wrongly and
by force, they put you in this place merely because you
preferred silence, everlasting silence, that day when you
decided to cut off your little tongue, that simple lump of
flesh with which you were always giving vent to words
and thoughts.

I shan't speak of this hellish place in which I am now
living; I shan't describe my feelings about the filthy grey

walls which keep me from sleeping, keep me staring up at the ceiling the whole night through, frightened they'll close in so tightly on me that they'll fall on to my body and shut off my breathing. I go on watching them drawing nearer and nearer, craftily stealing up on me until they are right close by me, at which I scream with all my strength, and then they move away from me and return again to their original positions. I shan't talk about that, nor about the fat lady with ugly little hairs scattered about under a chin rounded like the small egg of a serpent, as she bears down upon me and plunges her horrible injection in my backside, which, despite all the pain and the hatred, makes me laugh and guffaw so much that I make her enraged by having triumphed over her. I shan't speak of the filthy poisoned food they put before me every day and against which I have no right to protest. Once I wept long and bitterly when I saw a sparrow slip through the window and eat a few crumbs of it; I ran towards it to frighten it away but it had already picked up a small piece in its beak before flying away, a small piece of the poisoned food I eat. This made me weep bitterly for the whole day as I thought about the kind of miserable end that unfortunate sparrow would meet.

I shan't speak about all that, nor about many other things I have seen in this place, because thinking about such things makes me feel as though I have been tied to some enormous bomb that is about to blow up or, to be more exact, that is about to blow me up and scatter my brains and body into endlessly small fragments. I shall therefore confine myself to writing about what happened to me before I was forced into living in this place, when, one day some years ago, I began to feel there were things that were changing around me, had also in fact changed within myself, for ever since I graduated from the university and was appointed as an employee at the Water Company, a few drops from the flood had already made their appearance on the horizon, affecting both people and things, and even animals and plants.

This was the flood that came and which I saw sweeping over everything, everything of beauty in my beautiful city, so that on the very day they brought me to live in this frightful place, I was smiling tenderly and looking at the tall buildings scattered here and there, with the van passing through the streets at a crazy speed. I was smiling and saying: Farewell, farewell, my beautiful city, the flood has once again swept you away.

I first noticed signs of the flood in the street which I used to walk along on my daily journey from home to my job at the Water Company, that street I loved so much, was so proud of, and about which I felt so strongly because of being an inhabitant of the city in which it lay. Even at this moment as I sit down to write, a feeling of joy flashes through me and my heart is filled with yearning as I imagine the pictures made by the bright, laughing colours of the shop awnings, bright orange and sparkling blue, and that marvellous awning I used to gaze at so long while the vendor handed me the paper cone of monkey nuts, the awning of the 'Freedom Star' shop that sold chick-peas and all types of salted melon seeds and other things to munch and chew.

When the advance of the flood started, the street I had been familiar with since childhood, and along which I had walked so many times, began to change and little by little started to lose its landmarks. The glass of the clean bright shop windows in which, so brilliantly did they shine, one could of a morning see one's face, had begun to lose their lustre and grow dull, and the well-laid pavement damp with water during the hot hours of summer had come to be pitted with holes in which dirty water had collected, and I would notice that these holes were becoming larger day by day till they formed what looked like stagnant pools spread around the pavement. Making my way along the street daily, coming and going to work on foot, I would generally amuse myself by gazing at the street's beautiful little trees, and I would count them. I would know that after the blue gum tree there would be the casuarina, then the Indian fig, and some ten metres before arriving at the door of the Water Company there would be a beautiful tree whose name I never got to know, a tree with spreading branches almost all of whose leaves would fall at the coming of spring when it would be resplendent with a vast quantity of large purple flowers; it would look magnificent, a unique spectacle among the other trees. I knew by heart the number of trees along the way; thirty-one green-leafed trees adorning the street and bringing joy to my heart whenever I looked at them.

Then one day I counted them and found there were thirty. I was amazed and imagined I had miscounted because of being preoccupied with something else as I had been walking. But when I counted them again on my return from the Water Company at midday, I discovered that one of the nine Indian fig trees had disappeared from its place, it had been uprooted and thrown down on the pavement amidst the rubble from the old building they were pulling down. It looked to me like the dead body of some harmless bird that had been treacherously done to death without having committed any crime. I found myself weeping bitterly, for nothing but tears was of any use with that terrible lump stuck in my throat that made me feel I was about to be throttled. From that moment I began to sense changes taking place inside me: there were slight pains in my insides and I would constantly have frightful headaches. To begin with I didn't give the matter much thought, but things continued like this for days and weeks, and after a while the headache changed into ghastly pains in my head, crazy pains that accompanied every breath I took.

It was then that I went to the doctor, who began giving me sedatives and tranquillisers, though these had no effect. Eventually they diagnosed my condition as being a chronic inflammation of the large intestine brought about by nervous tension. When there were only three trees along the whole of the road, a mere three trees out of the thirty-one, I didn't know exactly what had come over me, nor what calamity had befallen my city or the people in it. All I remember about that period is that my weight went up enormously so that I was regarded as being obese, and that I had lost the capacity to be cheerful. No longer did I have any desire to go to the cinema or to converse with my women friends on any of the topics I used to talk about. I even made up my mind not to think about marriage at all, despite my getting on in years – though I might say that I was by no means ugly. Even after putting on weight as mentioned, I was still regarded by some people as possessing a certain beauty, maybe because of my good complexion, large eyes and soft hair. The truth was that during this period I was always thinking about one thing: how could I one day get married and bear children who would live in this city? What misery they would experience when they looked around them and found nothing but a vast jungle planted with concrete and colours of grey and brown! Also, I won't conceal the fact that I was even more afraid for my grandchildren, when I thought about what it would be like for them when they came out into the world and lived in this city, without seeing a flower or knowing the meaning of the word.

Besides, those who presented themselves as possible hus-
bands did not appeal to me in the least, maybe because I
would have liked a young man who was completely different from all the men I had come across in my life; a young
man who loved this city as I did and who wouldn't get
bored counting its trees on warm summer evenings when
the sky is clear and the moon shines down on the world
from on high. I would let my gaze wander far away and
would dream of my unknown young man who would
accompany me as we walked hand in hand in the city's
streets, chatting away as we ate monkey nuts.

Nevertheless I won't deny that I did go out one day
with a colleague of mine from work. There was a certain
simple affection between us that prompted us to do this.
On that day, the day I went out with him, he asked me
to sit with him at a riverside café and have a lemonade or
some other cold drink. I refused and said that I preferred
to sit right at the river's edge and watch the water as it
made its way aimlessly to the sea. I also said that I didn't
like lemonade. When I saw his dark eyes under the arched
eyebrows gleaming because of the golden rays of sunset,
making him look so handsome and gentle, at that moment
my heart missed a beat and, leaning over, I kissed him on
the lips. At this he got to his feet angrily, scolding me
harshly and asking why I had been so forward as to do
such a thing in a public place. At the time there was no
one there but an aged vendor of lupin seeds. I too became
angry, so we got up and parted in the large square, and
from that moment on I haven't talked to him.

What brought me to their notice and led to their putting
me here in this loathsome place, and what made me utterly
convinced that I was on one side and they on another,
had its beginnings in a day when I slept late because of a
beautiful dream in which I had seen that the trees of my

beloved street had all returned to where they had been; in fact they were all in leaf and flower and they had produced wonderful, fantastically shaped fruits of exquisite colours the like of which I had never seen before. Waking from my dream to the heat of the sun's rays falling on my forehead, I discovered that I would be very late for work. I therefore got up and dressed hurriedly, without having any food or drinking my usual glass of tea, and rushed along the street which I had now become used to seeing so dirty and crammed with cars and people. Suddenly, as I ran, I discovered that I had forgotten to put on my brassière. I felt embarrassed and upset and said to myself: How stupid of me! Fancy forgetting such a thing! I thought of returning home to put on the brassière, but this would have meant arriving too late to be able to sign in at the Water Company. So I continued on my way, saying that maybe no one would notice. It seemed to me that my not going back home that day confirmed everything that was said of me at the Company about being eccentric and not caring about my work.

I stopped for a while in front of a store which had put a large mirror behind the shoes it was displaying in the window, and I gazed at myself and found that my breasts seemed to be hanging rather loosely. I said to myself: And what's the harm in that? and I went on my way again thinking about brassières and who had invented them and what was the significance or the point of them. And when I had thought and thought I came to the conclusion that it was a funny piece of clothing, really funny, and that women were stupid to insist on putting their breasts into them every day. Also, what was so shameful about a woman's breasts?

When I got to work, and after about an hour of doing some of the routine accountancy work, I went to the chief's office for him to sign some papers. I noticed that when he stretched out his hand to take them from me he was overcome by a sudden fit of embarrassment and that the tips of his ears began to go a bright red, after which he started to sweat profusely. As this was the end of autumn and it was early morning, I was afraid the man might be ill. 'Anything wrong with you, Mr Aziz?' I said. 'Shall I bring you a glass of water?' He answered me with a brusqueness I had not known in him, I who had been accustomed to being treated by him with such kindness and gentleness, for I am, as he always used to say, very sensitive. He asked me to leave and to return to my office and said that he would summon me in a little while.

However, after a while, he called for my colleague Nadia, who is senior to me in both age and rank. No sooner had she left his office than she came towards me, with flushed face, and asked me, as she scrutinized me, to follow her as she would like to have a word with me in the corridor by the toilets. Once there she glared at me and began rebuking me: 'How dare you,' she said, 'come to work without a brassière?' and she informed me that this behaviour had greatly upset Mr Aziz and that he regarded it as a dangerous precedent in the company which he could not pass over in silence and that he would punish me for behaving in an indecent manner. I became quite frantic and almost slapped her heavily made-up face.

I then ran off to Mr Aziz's room and said to him, trembling with rage and exasperation, that I had in fact forgotten to put on a brassière, determined as I was to arrive at the Water Company at the time laid down. I also informed him that I had decided from now on to turn up at the Water Company without a brassière because I had given a lot of thought to brassières and had found that there was no need for such a piece of clothing, in the same

19

way that there was absolutely no sense to the necktie he was wearing. There was a large number of male and female colleagues gathered in Mr Aziz's room and for the first time I heard such whisperings as: 'She's not normal! She's mad!'

Before the mishap mentioned there had been various other small incidents, but in none of them did I clash with a boss or colleague. I used to avoid all of them and would converse with them only within the most narrow limits and on matters relating solely to my work. I would save up the thoughts and opinions I had formed about the streets and people for one of the most pleasurable times of the day: those minutes before going to sleep during which I would always feel a clarity of mind and cleanliness of spirit that made me think about my own life and the lives of the people in this city. Once the thought came to me: Why is there all this filth at the Water Company? Why is the colour of the desks always a gloomy grey? Also, why is it that so many files and heaps of papers are stacked up in corners to form a nightly playground for insects and rats? An idea came to me which I expected would be a happy surprise for everyone: having saved up several pounds from my salary, I bought a beautiful desk and asked the man I'd bought it from to paint it a bright red and to send it addressed to me at the Water Company.

I went to work early on the day the desk was to be delivered and began cleaning up the accounts room in which I sat with six of my colleagues: I swept it and polished it and cleaned the windows, then placed on the desk of each employee a pretty bunch of flowers in a glass of water. At noon the man came to the Company to deliver my red desk, but the security officer who was in charge of who was allowed in and out refused to let in the man with my red desk. However, after the man had shown him the bill with my name written on it, he contacted the company manager, who immediately summoned me. He asked me what it was about and I said to him: 'Why do we have to have grey desks? What would be wrong if one employee were to be seated at a red desk, another at a green desk, and a third at a yellow desk, and so on? Wouldn't this make everyone feel jolly?' He looked at me in amazement, at which I said to him: 'I bought the desk out of my own money and when I've saved some more money I'll buy some simple pieces of furniture for the accounts room.'

The man, whom I still dislike right up to this very day, looked at me scornfully and said: 'Go back to your office.' Then he ordered the security officer not to allow the desk to be brought in. At this the blood boiled in my veins and I began shouting: 'This isn't fair! Why do you think in this way? What's wrong with a red-coloured desk?' and I was so upset that I had a slight fainting fit, after which they took me home.

Until now I have been speaking of trifling matters. I have spoken about some things but not about all of them. Now I shall tell exactly how it was that they brought me, wrongly and by force, to this place. It was on the day they decided to hold general elections in the city. I went along to cast my vote, for, as a citizen of full legal age, I had to make a point of exercising my constitutional right. However, the problem that kept worrying me, as I was on my way to vote, was purely and simply that I did not know exactly who was the proper candidate to vote for. I went on turning the matter over in my mind. The fact was that, being quite interested in public affairs, I used to attend several discussion groups held here and there that dealt with such matters, and once, when I was still at school, I marched in a demonstration acclaiming the

Algerian Revolution and Jamila Buhairid,* and every day I used to devote myself to assiduously reading the newspaper, but none of this led me to the candidate for my vote.

As I was walking along one of the streets leading to the elementary school where the election committee was to be found, I noticed a weasel warily sticking its head out from the doorway of one of the closed shops, then scurrying across the street in the direction of the school. I stopped for a while and thought about the scene I had witnessed a few minutes ago. What did it mean? What was it all about? A weasel in the full light of day?! I couldn't control my feelings as I thought about it, for this was not the first time I had seen this small animal with the dejected face and soft, lithe body roaming through the streets of the city. I had seen it many times before crossing the streets, coolly going wherever it pleased. My violent headache had me in its grip and the chronic pains I used to suffer from played their mad tunes in my stomach, a stomach that had become as inflated as that of a pregnant woman. I sat down on the edge of the pavement in a state of semi-collapse, crying bitterly.

Some people came along and began to calm me down. An old woman said, 'There is no power or strength except through Allah,' as she patted me on the shoulder, while I answered their enquiries as to what was wrong. All I could say was, 'Nothing . . . nothing.' Then I got up, stopped crying and continued on my way until I reached the elementary school.

What happened after that? I don't know exactly. There were many people there and one of them gave me some

*A heroine of the Algerian Revolution who was arrested and tortured by the French.

papers which I read without understanding anything. Someone else was hanging up various pictures and patterns, such as a palm-tree, a dog, a camel, a watch and other such things.* It seems one of them noticed I was reading the pieces of paper with interest, so he came up to me and began a conversation. Then he indicated that I should vote for the candidate to whose party he belonged, so I enquired: 'Does your party do anything about planting trees in the city instead of concrete? Has it formed a well-equipped army to deal seriously with the weasels? Does it possess some medicine that can restore my good spirits?' The discussion circle began to grow as some people joined in, and after a lot of talking and arguing I said to them: 'It's quite futile what you're all doing, with your bodies as flabby as they are, for a healthy mind is in a healthy body. Apart from which, most of our ministers are ugly and they have such fat necks one doubts their ability to do anything useful.' Then in a loud voice I enquired: 'Where are the women? I see no women around me. Why have you not sought out the reasons for the sparrows having fled from our city and why is it so full of flies and mosquitoes?' They began guffawing with laughter and some of them moved away. One man, however, asked me in a commanding tone to go inside the building with him for a while. When I asked him why, he scowled at me. I paid him no attention, and when he demanded to see my identity and voting cards, I produced them in all good faith. He took them from me and refused to give them back. I cursed him and started to hit him, at which I suddenly found some of the people attacking me. I called out for the police and for those in charge,

---

*To help illiterate voters candidates are given such symbols.

after which I was aware of nothing until I found myself back home.

On the following day they brought me here, where I am now. How did this happen? I had come to at the beginning of the night to find myself in my bed, with a terrible headache and feeling exhausted. I found my mother giving me anxious, angry looks and saying to me, 'Have things come to such a state with you? Have you reached the stage when you'll ruin the future of your brother? Do you not know that he is an officer and that this behaviour of yours may force him to leave his work? Won't you ever stop your silliness and keep silent? By Allah, you deserve to have your tongue cut out.' Then she began crying and left the room.

After that I stayed for a while staring up at the ceiling thinking about what she'd said. I went over it word by word and felt that I was truly in the wrong, that it was criminal of me. How could I have done such a thing without taking into account how it might affect my brother's sensitive position in his job? How could I heedlessly have done something to harm him? Suddenly there came into my mind an image of myself when small and of my mother threatening to cut off my tongue with a pair of scissors because I had divulged a secret to my father, directly on his return from work, which was that my brother had broken a china vase in the sitting room while playing with a ball. My mother had taken up the scissors after my father had gone out to the café at sunset and had trapped me in a corner of the room. She had then opened them wide and had approached me menacingly, asking me to put my tongue right out so she could cut it off and stop it from divulging any more secrets. I was screaming with terror and pleading with her not to do it. Then I expressed my regret and apologies for what I had done, while my young brother stood watching me and laughing.

I was remembering this as I continued staring up at the ceiling. What, I thought, would have happened if my tongue had actually been cut off? Would not all my difficulties have ended there and then? Would I not have kept silent for ever? I would have contented myself with watching what went on around me without expressing any opinion or saying anything. Is not this less dire than suicide? Previously I had often thought about committing suicide, and on one occasion I had tried to cut a vein in my hand with a razor blade, but at the last moment I had drawn back, firstly because I had been afraid of dying, and secondly because I was afraid of dying an unbeliever and never being accepted into heaven. At the time, though, I was more afraid of the pain and so had changed my mind. But one's tongue is a different matter; cutting it off did not mean I would die, I would merely be losing the ability to articulate. I was in a state of great tension and agitation as I arrived at that point in my thinking. So I got out of bed and stood in front of the mirror, then gazed at the strange image of my face which now constantly had dark circles round the eyes. I looked at the yellowness of my complexion, then put my tongue so far out that I could see my uvula. I found it to be long and wide and a deep red colour. I said: 'Fear nothing, dear tongue, you are but a small piece of flesh. There will be a little blood and, of necessity, some pain, then all your pains will be over for ever' – and I remembered my circumcision operation when I was nine and I said to myself: Never mind! I stretched out my hand to the scissors lying on the dressing-table below the mirror and opened them out wide, as my mother had done one day in the past, and placed my tongue between the blades.

Where in the Devil's name did my mother appear from at that moment to snatch the scissors away from me? I don't know exactly, only that I suddenly found her in front of me, bearing down and snatching them from me, then screaming and wailing so that the neighbours and people from the street gathered. After a while they took me off to this place. I do not know how long has gone by since I was first lodged here, maybe many years. But my mother, who used to visit me a lot and who would talk to me without my replying to her, no longer comes at all. As for my brother, who has been visiting me at infrequent intervals, he says nothing. I have told my story without avail to all the nurses and doctors around me who merely smile and pat me on the back; I tried to make them understand that I was thinking of cutting off my tongue so that I might stop talking and avoid trouble, but this has been of no use.

And here I am now writing these words. Perhaps some person will read them and learn the truth about me, the truth about my being unfairly treated and put in this place, wrongly and by force. I am writing this because of my growing feeling that I am at the point of death, for my body has withered, my hair gone white and my legs are no longer able to carry me. Yet I hope to get out of this place, be it even for a single hour, that I may see my city and the road so dear to my heart, which I have so often walked along and in which at such time I would so hope to see thirty-one beautiful green trees.

3

The Sorrows of Desdemona

Mrs Inayat came up to her and touched her head with the palms of her hands, causing her to bend forward, and said in her English that seemed as though it had been running in her blood for generations, 'No, not like that, Muna. Desdemona couldn't be like that in this situation. Be more frightened, more submissive and miserable, with your head like this – bent forward.'

She continued to draw deeply on her cigarette as she followed the scene. She was like a butterfly sipping at the nectar of a flower. She was an unforgettable woman, one that became engraved on one's memory: not merely her features but that strange way she was formed, making her different from other women. She resembled no one, was like no one, Muna told herself as she delivered Desdemona's long monologue. If only she were my mother, or if only my mother were like her. If only I were able to approach her, to talk to her. During the lessons she looks like a priestess in some temple. Everyone keeps reverently quiet, out of respect, and silence and peace reign. If only all women were like her. How lovable she is!

27

Suddenly Muna stopped and said to Mrs Inayat in a whisper, 'I'm going to the bathroom.'

Mrs Inayat gave a little laugh that brought together tens of tiny lines in a network at the corners of her eyes, and her lower lip made a droll, good-natured movement as she said, 'Fine. Hurry back.'

Muna meant to say to her that she had to go because the hook of her brassière had come undone, but instead she hurried out of the stage hall into the wide school courtyard strewn with sand. She crossed to the end of it, passing by the classrooms till she reached the lavatories. Everything was calm, totally unrelated to the noisy morning life of the school, and she thought about how much she hated the school and the lessons, the cramped classrooms and having to stand in line every morning. She also hated the Arabic language teacher, with his boorishness and corpulence and dirty, yellow teeth and the way he revelled in explaining the reasons why polygamy was allowed. Suddenly she found herself spitting on to the sand and burying it under her shoe. Her father, too, was like the Arabic language teacher; she hated him when he ate with such relish at lunch and sipped noisily at his tea, then got up and made his ablutions and prayed; then, after performing his prayers, staying on and muttering to himself, taking up the newspaper in one hand and the transistor radio in the other and making off to his room while her mother followed after him like a dog following its master. She thought that Mrs Inayat wouldn't do that; in her home she imagined her as being completely different, though she didn't know exactly in what way. She looked like some wonderful saint painted on an old Coptic icon. Muna remarked to herself about Mrs Inayat's eyes. It was when she had looked hard at her of late during the rehearsals for the play, something she didn't have the opportunity of doing during class as Mrs Inayat would generally be busy writing on the blackboard or looking into a book, that Muna had discovered that her eyes did not possess a single, clearly defined colour. To begin with she had thought them to be dark brown, but yesterday, when the sun had wheeled westwards and its rays had suddenly fallen through the hall window onto Mrs Inayat's raised face, she had discovered that her eyes were as light-coloured as the yellow of honey and that they glistened like crystal, thus giving her a new beauty that itself possessed the sweetness of honey. She thought to herself: What sort of woman is this whose eyes are so differently coloured that they look as deeply black of an evening as her sorrows at things inscrutable and unknown and which so seldom permit her to laugh or smile?

Having reached the lavatory, Muna began undoing the buttons of her white school blouse. When she turned round and faced the mirror her breasts looked prominent and widely spaced under the unfastened brassière. Taking it off, she continued to gaze at her breasts. An obscure sensation pervaded her, reaching right down to the tips of her feet. She raised her hand and passed her palm over her neck and breasts; with her fingers she touched the small rosy nipples. She gave a sigh of pleasure, and while she was fixing that small piece of cloth with the elastic straps, it suddenly came to her that Mrs Inayat didn't wear a brassière. For some moments she remained overwhelmed by her utter astonishment at this discovery. She told herself that Mrs Inayat's breasts moved with complete freedom, swaying about as they pleased under her roomy dress. This was evident whenever she moved or bent down. Though she didn't know what this discovery meant in relation to herself, she smiled and stood for a moment thinking that she too would do that, that it would be wonderfully comfortable. But she had a feeling of fright when she remembered that were her mother to see her like that, it would take on all sorts of meanings and that she would scold her for spoiling her breasts by allowing them to sag. She gave a groan as she adjusted her breasts inside the small lace cavities, staring at the ceiling as she did up the buttons of her blouse. Then she ran out into the empty courtyard.

When she entered, Mrs Inayat and the rest of the girls were at the far end. On seeing her coming, Mrs Inayat raised her voice so that it would carry across the vast hall, this time speaking in Arabic. 'Hurry up, you've been a long time and we're waiting for you.' Muna apologized and as she took her place she remembered that the sun was nearly setting. She felt depressed: she had to return home but she would so like to stay on, for these were the most beautiful moments she lived through, standing here with Mrs Inayat as she was about to start acting. She would feel she was a crowned queen and would behave with confidence, forgetting she was a seventeen-year-old student. Her fear of her mathematics mistress and of the biology master would fall away from her. These were the sole moments when she loved the school and the girls, and that sensation of constant loneliness would leave her. Though she now appeared stronger than anyone could imagine, yet she still had to return home. There they wouldn't understand about all this. Inevitably there would be a battle and her father would hit her and her mother would scold her.

At that instant Mrs Inayat was directing her gaze at the open window as she exclaimed in a loud, excited voice, 'That was what Desdemona's feelings were – a mixture of fear, pain and contempt. She was suffering just like a sparrow that is incapable of battling against the wind. Do you understand? Listen: human beings can express such pain in many ways. Now close your eyes and for three minutes think about Desdemona's sorrows and how you'd express such pain. Come on, let's begin.' She closed her eyes and all the girls closed theirs and their features relaxed.

Muna too closed her eyes and thought about Desdemona's sorrows, saying to herself that her young brother would open the door and scream 'Muna's come!' He would point to his throat with a quick gesture as though someone were cutting the throat of a chicken and would stick his tongue out gloatingly. As soon as the door closed her mother would be in the hallway, meeting her with abuse, and she would say that she had been at school in the group taking coaching in physics, and her father would shout out that he had the curriculum of the group and that there were no classes on a Tuesday. She would go on swearing to him that she was telling the truth, and he would shout and say he wasn't a liar, then he would go up to her and give her two slaps across the face. Of course as usual she wouldn't cry; she would look at him with contempt and her mother would drag her away by the hand, weeping and cursing fate which had afflicted her with daughters. In a histrionic moment her father would approach her in an attempt to strike her again, but her mother would entreat him by the beloved Prophet and his own virtuous mother not to do so, and she would heap more abuse on Muna, reminding her that her father was a sick man and that she'd bring about his death by such behaviour. She would want to scream, to utter long, endless groans, to weep, to throw up everything in her stomach.

She felt a burning fire in her throat, repeated explosions in her head. Her eyebrows knotted in fury, and her pursed

31

lips moved in quick, nervous twitches which, together with the grinding of her jaws, produced a soundless, destructive melody of sadness, anger and pain, a melody that was cut short by Mrs Inayat's calm voice, 'Muna, are you all right?'

With a sigh she answered: 'Yes, Mrs Inayat, thank you. Shall I begin first? I'm all right now.'

4

A Small White Mouse

The lights turned to red and the insane uninterrupted deluge of traffic came to a halt, allowing a surge of people to rush forward and hurriedly cross the street. This caused Husniyya to stand up straighter and raise her voice in a shout, 'Have a go and see your luck for a shilling.'

Over and over she repeated the call. When no one stopped by her, she threw a piece of dry bread into the cage of the mouse, who was looking on expectantly, then began once again to gaze at the traffic lights in anticipation of probable customers. Meanwhile her attention was taken up with the very same thoughts that had begun several days ago to harass her, and which up till this very moment still spoilt her life for her: 'Just suppose, my girl, Uncle Hasan recovered and was up and about, hale and hearty, it would be as if all your efforts had been for nothing. And what if Uncle Hasan agreed to bring you a work kit, when he's convinced you're intending to make your living in some place away off the map, the problem's still there, the same knot in the wood the saw can't deal with. Because the work kit costs money, it can be very expensive, and he'd take it out on you because you know he'd give his life for a piastre and can't easily part with money.'

She sighed with annoyance and extreme anger at her husband, feelings so intense that she imagined that, were he to appear before her at that instant, she would pick up the largest stone and hurl it at him to smash his head in and would also give him a good beating, because all the hardship she was living through was caused by him, he having left her in the position of some charitable endowment that can never be changed, neither divorcing her nor returning to her to take up her worries and make her feel she was someone living in the world like everyone else.

She felt that the world in her sight was narrower than the eye of a needle. She left the mouse in its cage on the cardboard box she used as a table and walked a few steps till she reached the boy sitting in front of a mat on which were scattered shoelaces, boxes of matches and plastic combs. Suppressing her feelings of exasperation, she said to him, 'Let's have a couple of puffs, by the Prophet, Abdurraheem.'

With a flamboyant gesture, which made him look like a miniature man, the boy took a long pull at the cigarette between lips that bore as yet no trace of a moustache, then he raised his head and handed her the cigarette, while his eyes roamed over the details of her body under the *galabia*, which appeared somewhat transparent due to the morning sunlight. Busying himself with arranging some small mirrors on the mat, he said to her, 'It's all yours.'

She thanked him, after having filled her chest with a long draught of smoke, and went back to the mouse. When she felt she had calmed down a little, she began calling out again, 'Have a go and see your luck for a shilling.'

Within a matter of seconds – she didn't know what

happened exactly – all hell broke loose. A huge grey van
came to an abrupt stop by the pavement and with light-
ning speed policemen and officers descended from it, after
which boxes of matches and tins of shoe polish, metal
keys and plastic shoes, nails and shoelaces, all went flying
about, and blows were mingled with shouts and with
people rushing about and screaming. The policemen were
scooping up the wares of the vendors with dazzling speed
and hurling them into the back of the huge grey van.
When Husniyya saw the white mouse making a complete
somersault in the air, complete with cage, then disappearing into the van, she was quite sure they must be the
government police. She slapped her breast and screamed
at the top of her voice, 'What a calamity!'

Madly she rushed off in the direction of the van in an
attempt to rescue the mouse, but all she got was a slap on
the face from a well-practised hand, which set her head
spinning. She began swearing and cursing, the tears
streaming from her eyes. Once again she tried to retrieve
the mouse, dashing forward and covering the hand of the
sergeant with both of hers, trying to stop him so she could
tell him that the mouse had been left in her safe-keeping
and that she was working with it for an old man, like
himself, who was ill. 'O God, may He keep you safe for
your children, sergeant, and protect you from the evils of
the highways. Give me back the mouse because it cost a
lot and it will be difficult to find another one like it.' She
told him she'd be forced to pay its price to its owner
because it was his only capital.

But the sergeant turned a deaf ear and violently withdrew his hand from between hers. 'Get away or I'll throw
you into the van to join your mouse,' he told her. He
busied himself collecting up the rest of the things left by
the vendors who had fled.

She stood watching and hitting herself on the head in desperation but before long, when she saw him lighting a cigarette and putting his hand in his pocket, an idea occurred to her. She went up to him and pushed ten piastres furtively into his hand, at the same time adjusting her head-scarf and whispering, 'May God keep you safe in every step you take . . . By the Prophet, let me have back the cardboard box.'

She stood waiting when he told her that he would do so when the officer had moved away a little so that he wouldn't be noticed. She tried to look unconcerned whenever an officer or a policeman passed in front of her, thinking about the people's things that the government had taken, things that were all they possessed and that they worked with in order to keep body and soul together. She was extremely surprised at how the government never stopped lying in wait for poor miserable folk, always picking on them over every blessed thing, and having no mercy on them and not even letting God's mercy descend on them, making problems because people may be standing around looking for charity, despite the fact that the road's plenty wide enough and people are going about as they wish, and the vendors haven't trodden on the government's toes in any way – not like the shopkeepers who fill up the streets and the pavements with their goods and their cars. She smacked her lips in disgust and brought to mind the proverb that says that he who doesn't have someone to back him will be beaten about the ears.

Suddenly it was as though an electric current had passed through her face: she had seen the sergeant returning from the van quite empty-handed. She hurried towards him enquiringly. 'The cage broke and the mouse escaped,' he told her.

All the joints of her body went slack and the blood in

her veins ran cold. Again she began striking her chest. 'Woe is me, mother!' she shrieked.

Then she sat down on the ground, crying and wailing, at which the sergeant advised her to leave the place quickly and make herself scarce because if the officer were to see her making such a fuss he'd get annoyed and would perhaps collect her up in the van with those who were being detained for not having identity cards, and perhaps he'd think up some charge to make against her and she'd be in a real mess. She leapt up in fright, looking like someone who's just had somebody die, and she went off dragging her feet, thinking about the disaster that had come to her from God knows where and which she'd never dreamt would happen, and wondering what she'd say to Uncle Hasan, her neighbour and owner of the mouse. She was the only one, from among all the neighbours who lived in the rooms of the house, whom he had trusted with the mouse, and with his money. When he had got ill and become bedridden, it was she he had asked to go out and seek her livelihood in the street with the mouse, as he had done, by telling people's fortunes through it. Things would be even more difficult for her when he learnt that she had gone against his instructions and hadn't stood with the mouse somewhere along the outer wall of the university but had got greedy and taken her stand on the pavement of the big street with the rest of the vendors. It was the boy Abdurraheem who had recommended this to her and had given her the impression she'd do better business in the new location because it was near the main road. Also, Uncle Hasan wouldn't believe the truth because only three days ago he had asked her about the month that was coming and, when she had told him that it was February, he had urged her to take courage and get a move on in the work because that meant the season had begun and the students' exams were approaching, which would result in their asking more and more to have their fortunes told.

She wept bitterly. She felt that the Lord had taken vengeance on her for having deducted for herself a little of the takings – during the days that had just passed she had hidden a quarter of a pound each time for herself and hadn't told Uncle Hasan about it. But this thought quickly flew from her head when she remembered how stingy and tight he was with her, and that, despite the fact that she had to stand the whole day, in the end all he would stretch out in his hand to her was fifty piastres – though he knew perfectly well that she wouldn't stint him in his demands. On returning late at night she would do his washing and would cook for him and feed him with her own hand, because his own had begun to shake and he had grown very weak, and, over and above that, she would put up with the things the women in the rest of the house said about her, because of her going in and out of his room. She kept silent because the position with Uncle Hasan was a thousand times better than previously when she used to go around on the buses peddling chewing gum and combs. At least she was now standing in one and the same place with the mouse and no longer heard dirty talk directed against her by the driver or ticket collector, poisoning her body every other minute, and was no longer exposed all day long to curses and harsh treatment.

A furnace was raging in her head as she made her way towards the house. Her sorrows seemed to be endless and if she had happened to meet her wretch of a husband at that moment she would have cut him into bits, would have made mincemeat of him, for it was he who had caused her all this torment she had lived through since he left her and disappeared. He had separated her from her family when he married her in the village years ago and brought her to this city in which one didn't know whether one was coming or going and where there wasn't a soul prepared to raise his eyes and look into the face of the person in front of him in the street. Her mother had died ages ago and it hadn't occurred to her husband even to ask about her because he hated her in the same way as she had hated him. As for Uncle Hasan, who was so kind to her and was the only person she had in this world, she would lose him forever from the moment she reached the house and told him she had lost his means of earning his daily bread and had allowed the government to make off with the mouse. Perhaps he would believe her when she swore to him by her mother's grave and told him that the mouse had escaped from the government but that the policeman hadn't found it. The trouble was that she had invested high hopes in Uncle Hasan and so put up with his bossing her about and endured patiently his many demands although they made her absolutely furious sometimes. She was dreaming one day of his conscience pricking him and his saying: 'If I die, Husniyya my girl, take everything I have because I've got no family and everything's in your hands, and you've got a better right to it than any other creature in the world – to the mattress and the blanket, and the chair and the rest of the things – because you're a good girl and you've been at my disposal and service just as though you were my own daughter, my own flesh and blood. As for the few piastres in the pocket of the *galabia*, you can have them to buy yourself a nice *galabia* and a new nylon nightgown.'

The tears streamed down even more as she remembered all that and she chewed at her lips in bitterness as she approached the door of the house. She thought about how she would open the conversation with Uncle Hasan, and she pictured to herself how he would look when he got to know and flew into a rage and would say to her: 'Get out of my sight, you accursed girl, you who spoil everything, you thief, you bringer of disasters. Your man left you because your face brings bad luck.'

She had reached the courtyard of the house and was crying more and more. She found a throng of people in front of Uncle Hasan's room, with the owner of the house standing and barring the door with her vast body. 'No one's to go near him,' she was saying, 'till the health inspector comes and writes the paper for him.'

When she saw Husniyya approach, the tears filling her eyes, she said to her in astonishment, 'Did you hear the news, Husniyya? You're a good sort, by the Prophet, coming so quickly. Give me the money you got so we can prepare what's required for the burial and take part in the funeral procession early tomorrow morning, God willing.' Then she turned to the rest of the neighbours and said, 'Not a soul is to touch anything belonging to Uncle Hasan, for we intend to sell his belongings, God willing, to pay off the months of rent he's owing me.'

5

Dotty Noona

Apart from her father and the officer, his wife and son, almost no one, when the question was asked at the office of the public attorney, knew Noona. The only exceptions were: Hasanein the seller of bread; Futeih the grocer; Salim the man who did the ironing; and the garbage man. The latter, on being questioned, said he had no idea at all about her features, because he was always concerned with looking at the rubbish bin when she used to hand it over to him for emptying into his basket each morning.

Everyone's statements conflicted on the question of her features, for while the officer was certain she was snub-nosed and that her upper jaw protruded slightly, his wife answered at the office of the public attorney, 'Did she have any features?' then added, 'She was a very dotty girl, very weird.' As for her father, he contented himself by saying, as he dried his tears, 'She would have been a lovely bride, a girl in a million' – and to prove to the government the truth of his statement, he produced from the inner pocket of his *galabia* a small golden earring with a blue bead, which was the total bridal gift presented by the future husband, whom she had never seen.

Even Noona herself didn't know her own features well. The most she knew was that the officer's son had beautiful black hair like his mother and a vast nose like that of his father, except that the latter's nose had small black specks scattered around on it. She had noticed them any number of times when he got excited and wrinkled it up as he exclaimed 'Check' in a voice hoarse and strangled with laughter to his opponent at chess.

In any case, the girl Noona was not concerned about her looks, which she often saw reflected on the surface of mirrors, either in the bedroom of the officer and his wife, or in their son's room, when she would enter to clean and tidy – quickly lest time flew and the school hours came to an end. She would snatch hurried moments in which to search yet again for 'the pupil of the eye', that being she never believed existed although the teacher had confirmed it over and over again. Each time, standing on tiptoe, she would crane forward with her short body and get as near as she could to the mirror, then would pull down her lower lids with her swollen fingers, which were covered with burn marks and small cuts, and in bewildered astonishment, get her eyes to bulge out, two black circles, while she peered around in search of two arms or two feet, or a nose or a neck, or any of the human parts of the body of that person, 'the pupil of the eye'. When, bored, tired and feeling that the tips of her feet had begun to ache because of her stance, she would lower herself, screw up her lips in rage, fill up her mouth with air, or put out her tongue and move it around in continuous circular movements, then go back quickly and start making the beds, hanging up the clothes and putting things in their proper places.

It is impossible to deny that the girl Noona had a secret desire to be pretty and charming, not like the officer's wife, who owned all sorts and kinds of clothes, something short and something long, and something with sleeves and something without sleeves, but pretty, like the teacher whom she used to imagine in the likeness of the fairy-tale princess whenever there came to her from beyond the window, while Noona stood in the kitchen, her beautiful voice asking the girls to repeat after her the hemistich, 'Flanks of antelope, legs of ostrich.'

'Flanks' used to puzzle Noona greatly, so when she began to repeat it with the girls and listen to the effect of her high-pitched solo voice declaiming 'flanks of antelope', she would stop for a while scouring the dish she was washing in the sink, or stirring what was cooking in its saucepan on the stove, and would rest her right leg against her left for a time and start sucking her thumb with relish as she thought about the real meaning of this 'flanks' and asking herself, Is it clover? Or candy with chick-peas? Or a young donkey?

The images burst forth in her imagination as she searched for the truth. When the questions defeated her and she discovered that water was beginning a trickle over the top of the sink, or that the cooking had boiled enough, she would apply herself again to her work, while rage and perplexity built up, a huge force within her body, and she would rub and scour the dishes till they were sparkling, or rearrange the spoons and forks in their places more neatly, while muttering the words 'legs of ostrich' and looking out of the window enclosed by the iron bars through which she could see the school building opposite, and the open blue sky sheltering it. There travelled up to her the voices of the girls in one strong harmonious sound, and she would feel that she was on the brink of madness,

43

and she would shout, along with them, with all the
strength of her throat, 'He lopes like a wolf, leaps like a
fox.'

She yearned to know the secrets of many other things,
things she had heard from this magical world hidden from
her behind the window, just as she longed to know the
true meaning of 'flanks', that word on which, through the
girls' school, she had made raids from time to time, and
which had made her learn by heart strange words she
didn't understand and made her wish she would find
someone to assuage her heart's fire and explain their meanings to her. She had in fact attempted to get to know the
meaning of these words by asking Hasanein the bread-
seller about 'flanks', but he had just winked at her and
raised his eyebrows obscenely and made a movement with
his thumb that reminded her of the village women.
Though she cursed him and reviled his father and his
scroundrelly ancestors, she was frightened after that to
make another attempt with Futeih the grocer. She would
have made the decision to ask the officer's son, if it hadn't
been for what occurred on the day of the square root,
which caused her never to think of it again. Surprised
one day by her mistress when stirring the onions and
scrutinizing them in her search for hydrogen sulphate,
which the teacher had said was to be found in them,
Noona adamantly refused to tell her the truth of the matter
when she asked her in surprise what she was doing. She
contented herself by saying that she was looking for something strange in the onions, which caused the officer's
wife to say in reference to this occasion – and numerous
other occasions – that Noona was dotty and weird and
that her behaviour wasn't natural, particularly when she
saw her jumping around in the kitchen, raising her legs
up high and extending them forwards, in exactly the same

way she had seen the girls do when they wore their long black trousers in the spacious school courtyard.

The lady used to say this about Noona and would add, whenever she sat among her women friends of an evening in the gilt reception room the like of which Noona reckoned the headman of her village herself couldn't possibly have seen, that the girl was a real work-horse and had the strength to demolish a mountain, despite the fact she wasn't more than thirteen years of age. She said she'd never throw her out of the house, despite her being mad, specially as maids were very few and far between these days and hard to come by.

Although this opinion didn't please Noona at all, and although the lady once slapped her on the face because of her having sworn at her young son and called him an idiot, she didn't dislike the officer's wife, for she knew that the slap had been a spontaneous reaction, just as Noona's swearing had been.

The boy had been sitting in the living room with the teacher, with his mother seated opposite them knitting and making cracking noises with her chewing-gum, when Noona came in carrying the tea-tray just as the teacher was asking the boy about the square root of twenty-five and the good-for-nothing was picking his nose and looking at his mother stupidly and giving no answer. As Noona had heard a lot from the schoolmistress about square roots, she couldn't help herself, when suddenly the boy brazenly answered four, from shouting in excitement, just as the schoolmistress used to do, 'Five, you idiot,' which almost caused the tray to fall from her hands. The teacher guffawed in amazement, and the boy ran towards her trying to hit her. The mother, however, got there first, for she had been concerned about the crystal glasses breaking, and had slapped Noona: the one and only slap she had given her during the three years she had been in the house. And whereas the lady didn't lie when she said to the teacher that Noona had no doubt heard that from the schoolmistress, one window looking right on to the other, Noona learnt never to talk about such things with anyone in the house lest the lady might think of dismissing her, for she wished to remain forever where the schoolmistress and the girls were, that beautiful world whose sounds she heard every day through the kitchen window, a world she never saw.

Despite all this there was a fire of longing that burned night and day in her breast for her mother and her brothers and sisters, and a desire to run about with the children in the fields, to breathe in the odour of greenness and the dewy morning, to see the blazing sun when she went out each morning, to hear the voice of her mother calling to her, when she was angry and out of sorts, 'Na'ima, Na'ouma, come along and eat, my darling, light of your mother's eyes.'

She used to love her real name Na'ima, also her pet name Na'ouma, but found nothing nice about the name Noona which had been given to her by the lady and by which everyone called her from the time of her arrival at the house from the country up until the time she left it for ever on that day after which nothing more was known of Noona. Before that her life had been going along in its usual routine: she had woken as was her habit, had brought the bread, had made breakfast for the officer, his wife and son, had handed over the tin container to the garbage man and had entered the kitchen after they had all gone out. It wasn't until about four o'clock that her life began to change when there was a knock at the door and Abu Sarie, her father, put in an appearance in order to drop his bombshell. After saying hello and having lunch and tea, and assuring her about her mother, and about her brothers and sisters one by one, and chewing the cud with her for a while, her father had said, as he eyed her breasts and body and smiled happily so that his black teeth showed, that he had come to take her back because she was going to be married. He showed her the gold earring that had been bought for her by the husband-to-be, who had returned from the land of the Prophet bearing with him enough money to furnish the whole of a room in his mother's house, and more besides. At that moment Noona's heart had sunk down to her heels and she had been on the point of bursting into tears. Smiling as he saw the blood drain out of her face and her colour become like that of a white turnip, Abu Sarie told her not to be frightened, for this was something that happened to all girls and that there was no harm in it. He asked her to make herself ready because they would be going off together next morning. Then he decided to make her happy with the same news that had made him happy, so he informed her that the lady would give her an additional month's wages as a bonus, also two pieces of cloth untouched by scissors, and that her younger sister would take her place in the job, if God so willed it.

'And everything was normal that night' – so said the officer's wife at the public attorney's office. Her husband and son both agreed with her, and even Abu Sarie himself. Noona had prepared supper, had washed up the dishes, had given the boy tea while he was studying in his room – 'and there was nothing about her to arouse one's suspicions,' she added – and this was in fact so. What happened was that Noona spent the night in her bed in the kitchen without having a wink of sleep, staring up at the dark ceiling and from time gazing towards the window behind which stood towering the school building, with above it a piece of pure sky in which stars danced. She was in utter misery, for she did not want to return to the village and to live amidst dirt and fleas and mosquitoes; she also did not want to marry, to become – like her sisters – rooted in suffering. The tears flowed that night from her eyes in rivers, and she remained sleepless till dawn broke. She saw with her two eyes the white colour of the sky and the black iron of the window, but by the time the lady called out to her to get up and go to the market to buy the bread, sleep had overcome her. She dreamed of the schoolmistress and the girls, and of the officer's son who, in her dream, she was slapping hard because he didn't know the square root of twenty-five. She also saw 'flanks', and it was something of extreme beauty; she didn't know whether it was a human or a *djinn*, for it seemed to be of a white colour, the white of teased cotton, with two wings in the beautiful colours of a rainbow. Noona seized hold of them and 'flanks' flew with her far away, far from the kitchen and from the village and from people, until she was in the sky and she saw the golden stars close to, in fact she almost touched them.

Those who had seen Noona on the morning of that day mentioned that her face had borne a strange expression. Both the officer and his wife said so, confirming that the look in her eyes was not at all normal when she had handed her master his packet of cigarettes as he was about to go out and when her mistress had asked her to straighten her kerchief before going to buy the bread.

The officer's wife was heard to say, with many laughs, to her women friends, after having told them the story of Noona, as she sat with them in the large living room, 'Didn't I tell you – she was crazy and altogether dotty? But as for her sister, I can't as yet make her out.'

6

An Occasion for Happiness

That day was not some big feast, nor a little one, nor was it some wedding celebration, yet a state of such extreme readiness had been announced since early morning that the father of Fawziyya – she had been so named because she had been born on the day when Princess Fawziyya had been married to the Shah of Iran – took things easy and didn't go to the government department as usual, he who never took any days off, even for sickness, except in extreme circumstances. Having made up his mind, he inclined to the opinion of his wife which held that 'time was short, it was winter, meaning to say that the day – in the name of God the merciful, the compassionate – was possessed of demons, so you'd no sooner had breakfast and cleared away the table than the noon call to prayer was saying "God is great" and the day was over.' Thus everyone woke early, had a bite to eat with tea, then Fawziyya's father went off to the barber for a haircut and a shave. Fawziyya's mother went about her business and began getting the lunch ready and doing her eyebrows, then took the children off to the bathroom. As for

Fawziyya herself – who was called Fawz for short – she had gone, after having a bath, to Hagga Ameena on the fourth floor of the building, and the clever woman had ironed out her coarse textured hair and shaped it into large lozenges, employing for the purpose a number of pencils, so that it looked shiny and beautiful with its dark brown colour, while her small head resembled, from afar, that of the queen who had had her head chopped off – Marie Antoinette. In addition to rendering this excellent service, Hagga Ameena, that good neighbour – all thanks to her – was kind enough to lend Umm Fawziyya her black overcoat with the six buttons, whose huge collar was made of rabbit fur in black and white, and Umm Fawziyya had taken care to fix on one side a clasp of imitation diamonds in the shape of the famous Statue of Liberty.

Until about five o'clock no important events worth mentioning occurred, apart that is from Fawz's family getting down to devouring the hen and the cock which her mother had killed in celebration of this happy occasion. In truth she would sooner or later have killed them anyway, even without any occasion to celebrate, because the hen had begun to eat her eggs directly she had laid them, and all stratagems to make her turn over a new leaf and desist had failed; as for the cock, despite the fact that he was now getting on in years and had lived sufficiently long, he had nevertheless not given up activities that caused tumult and mischief on the roof, and continued to insist on waging unsuccessful battles with another more youthful cock. In addition, Fawz took it upon herself to deliver a plateful of *basbousa* to Hagga Ameena from the dish her mother had made in celebration of her contentment and happiness on this memorable day.

Except for these two occurrences the remainder of the events took concrete form in the shape of a dream in the mind of Fawz's young brother, who pictured his sister's prize being a large and magnificent gun, and in, another fantasy, a small and ordinary one, perhaps a pistol that squirted water. The pictures went on pursuing one another in his mind in an uninterrupted sequence right up to the moment when his sister would kiss him and say, 'Take it, it's yours, Hasan, because I'm a girl and I don't like playing with guns and pistols.' He would thank her and rush away with the prize, running to the street to show it off to all the children who would implore him to let them play with it a little, or even just touch it, and he would refuse and would look with contempt at all their silly guns and pistols made out of pieces of old wood and clothes pegs, and would make fun of their ammunition which consisted of no more than date pits picked up off the ground of the lane.

As for Fawz's father, he wasn't – quite contrary to his son – thinking of anything material: all he hoped for was a sum of money, at the very least three pounds, to keep himself and the household going till the end of the month. There had been gradually growing within him a feeling as to the justice of his logic with the time approaching five o'clock, especially as his enthusiasm for this occasion had waned somewhat, perhaps by reason of the chicken in which he had rather over-indulged, perhaps because he had been irresponsible during the day, in spending on things that were unnecessary: the barber's, which he could have postponed, and Fawz's new shoes, in addition to the dish of *basbousa* which could have been dispensed with by making do with tea after lunch instead of a sweet.

At that time Fawz's mother was taking a bath to crown her efforts expended throughout the day. While she was scrubbing the calves of her legs, the veins of which were swollen from so much drudgery and standing about, and was singing in a hoarse voice, 'He brought me the clogs in the passenger train', she went on repeating to herself from time to time, smacking her lips in the vain hope: 'Oh, if only Fawziyya's prize were something useful for the house.' As for this useful thing, it could be one of countless articles, beginning with a woollen blanket to keep her old bones warm in winter, and ending up with a beautiful leather bag for Fawz instead of the linen duffel bag which she wore every day over her shoulder when she went to school. The fact was that Fawz herself didn't give the present much thought, being busy and happy with all the preparations allocated to her. Her enthusiasm and excitement at this occasion had reached the point where they had made her cheeks ruddy for the first time in the history of her life, for she was at all times pasty-faced and of a weak constitution, perhaps by reason of the breakfast she used to have which consisted usually of bread dipped in tea, or because she used only rarely to eat meat and fruit, for, like everybody else, she only saw any human being with rosy cheeks in advertisements or the colour magazines.

At around five the Fawz family procession set off, and with them Khadiga, the neighbours' daughter, who was allowed, by the invitation card, to accompany them. The invitation was confined to five persons, otherwise they would have taken all their friends and neighbours, all those who knew that Fawz was to be presented with a prize from the school. They stood looking out of the windows and doors admiringly, while Fawz's mother walked quietly along beside her husband, who proceeded with erect carriage and Hitler moustache, which he continued to wear, perhaps as a living reminder of the atroci-

ties of the Second World War in which he had not participated other than to hide himself in the stairwell with the
rest of the neighbours at the time of the raids. Fawz was
truly radiant in her blue tafetta dress, which still retained
its splendour despite the fact that it had been originally
one of her mother's, which she had been unable to get
into after she'd got too fat and put on weight through
becoming pregnant and giving birth. It could be said that
Fawz felt, for the first time in her life, that she was grown-
up and that she must be sensible and respectable and talk
in a subdued voice, as her mother always asked of her,
and not play hopscotch in the lane. This feeling had
increased with her after she had contemplated herself in
the mirror and ascertained how attractive she was, with
her hair all arranged and her eyebrows trimmed. There
was none the less one thing that worried her and that was
the new and over-large shoes that slightly impeded her
movements. Her mother had insisted on buying them
with plenty of room so that they might do for the coming
year, owing to the way in which Fawz's feet kept on
growing unrestrainedly. Her mother had stuffed four
pages of a coloured feature article from the magazine *Akhir
Sa'a* into them, two in each shoe at the toe, but the poor
thing still had to drag her feet along the ground and wasn't
able to skip and jump around with any ease, but in general
this small matter didn't greatly affect Fawz's spirits. She
remained very cheerful, so much so that as soon as they
arrived at the school she left them all in order to join
up with her fellow students who would be giving the
performance of music and dancing at the party. As for
her relatives and Khadiga, they had gone to take their
places. Their bottoms had hardly touched the chairs before
they were sitting up straight because the curtain was rising
and, while a respectful silence reigned for the national

53

anthem, the orchestra was striking up 'The eagle of Egypt has risen and long may it be high'. After that was over the presenter of the show came forward to announce that the programme would begin with the best and greatest of words, at which a Qur'an reciter came and sat on a high gilded chair placed on a platform and began chanting, 'And which is it of the favours of your Lord that you deny?' His voice was exceedingly moving, and Fawz's brother nudged his mother and enquired in astonishment: 'Has grandpa died once again?' As for the next item, it consisted of a word from the distinguished teacher, headmistress of the school – as the presenter announced – at which the distinguished lady hurried forward. She was one of those elderly women who had been denied marriage because of the clause in the law relating to education which absolutely forbade spinsters, on pain of being dismissed from their jobs, to marry. Having briefly greeted and thanked those present, she expounded the aim of the gathering and the importance of the role of education at this momentous stage in the life of the Egyptian people and then, arriving at the main subject of her address, abused imperialism and Zionism and hailed the heroic city of Port Said which had withstood the treachery of three nations. When everyone clapped warmly at that point, she added to what she had said and repeated it, and the people again clapped. Then she called upon the Most High, the Omnipotent, to protect the revolution and its leader, and everyone knew that the speech was drawing to its close. She didn't disappoint them, concluding with 'And peace be upon you and the mercy of God and His blessings.' There was some lukewarm clapping, followed by mutterings blended with the coughs of smokers and the bawling of babies which didn't stop when the curtain went up again almost at once to reveal Fawz with the girls and boys to sing: 'Shut up, London, shut up . . . Let Paris too shut up.' As her brother knew the rest of the song, and it appeared that many of the children had heard it before, a chorus of voices joined those of the singers on the stage: 'And let's go build the dam . . . and ask nothing of anyone.' Good cheer and joy showed on the people's faces, and Fawz's mother's eyes filled with tears from emotional excitement, while the items that had been rehearsed for the party followed one after the other. The public's enthusiasm was fired and reached its peak when a young girl with a deep voice sang, 'O treacherous Zionist . . . I'd sacrifice my eyes for Palestine.' The men clapped and the women uttered high trilling cries, and Fawz's father, as he sat there, began jogging his thighs up and down violently, a habit he had when excited. His son, sitting next to him, was upset about this and for a few short moments imagined his father would hit his mother.

At last came the moment for the distribution of the prizes. Everyone fell silent in expectation. Heads gazed fervently at the back door to the stage from where the headmistress would make her appearances to announce the names of the outstanding pupils and give each one his prize.

A disagreeably long period of time passed. It is not important to recount what occurred during it except to say that eventually everyone left the school, with Fawz's father walking in the street with sluggish steps, thinking of the necessity of buying some more medicine for his stomach pains, to replace that which was finished, and that he had a need to sleep with his wife that night, mainly because he couldn't clear his head of the image of that woman in the spotted red dress sitting close by with one leg over the other and exposing to view her two white knees. So he began stroking his wife's arm which was gripping his own in case she should fall because the heel of her shoe had begun to upset her balance slightly. Behind them walked Fawz's brother screaming and crying and demanding that they carry him because he wanted to go to sleep and at the same time cursing Khadiga and accusing her of having trodden on his foot. As for Fawz, she was staring ahead indifferently, thinking about taking her courage in both hands and asking her mother to buy them halva for supper. She was, meanwhile, carrying a small copy of the Qur'an on the inner cover of which was written: 'To the diligent pupil Fawziyya Mohammed Farid for her excellent performance in the end-of-the-year examination.' Below this was a printed seal with the emblem of the Republic, then the name of the distinguished teacher, headmistress of the school, and her signature.

7

That Beautiful Undiscovered Voice

Everything had started quite naturally in accordance with the usual daily rites: the rooms were tidied and cleaned, the plates were laid awaiting the food, the radio, turned down low, was chattering out the afternoon news, which in general was the same as usual. Abdul Hamid, however, felt that there was a certain unease affecting his wife, causing her to hunch her shoulders more than usual when she swallowed her food; also she was not entering into the conversation with him as she should.

'What is it, Sayyida?' he asked her.

'Nothing,' she replied glumly and went off to the kitchen, pleading that the tea was boiling over. But when she returned she seemed even more distressed and allowed the top of the teapot to fall on the floor as she was pouring the tea into the glasses. Abdul Hamid again asked her what was wrong in a disapproving tone. She shyly whispered back that she wanted to talk to him about something, but that she was embarrassed.

'Hope it's all right,' he said as he lit a cigarette, guessing at what the news would be. She would no doubt be asking for money and would give as a reason some incidental matter, or would try to persuade him that the monthly expenses had gone up. There was no other subject Sayyida would be embarrassed to talk about. He bared his teeth and knotted his brows and moved his neck from left to right so as to make a cracking noise as he prepared himself for the inevitable battle. He decided that he would come out the victor, however heated it was, for he was not going to pay one single red millieme over and above what he was already paying in household expenses each month, not if Sayyida – as the saying goes – were to see her own earlobe. He took a sip of the almost black tea, and said to her between clenched teeth. 'Out with it!'

From deep down inside her Sayyida tried to thrust her courage up to her tongue and to utter what she wanted to say, but her courage quickly slipped back again into its abyss. Her voice emerged weak and timid.

'The fact of the matter is I've discovered I'm . . .'

'Pregnant?'

The husband was on his feet, screaming, like someone who has of a sudden accidentally impaled himself. The words, 'Can it possibly be?' sprang from his lips, accompanied by a spray of spittle brought about by his agitation. 'Is it possible that you can again be pregnant, Sayyida? By my mother's grave, I'll be really annoyed with you if it's true, and my pocket's empty, which is to say no more children and, no more abortions. You get yourself out of this one, if you can.'

He gave himself a good scratch between the thighs and walked, crazed, towards the window, which overlooked the street filled with the clamour of people and cars. Enraged, he thought of what he might do to her. Should he hit her? Throw her to the ground and kick her till she started bleeding and had a miscarriage? Or should he open the window full and throw her out? If it hadn't been that the cigarette was almost burning his fingers, so that he had to return to bury the stub in the ashtray, Sayyida may not have found the opportunity, her courage having risen to her tongue, to say to him, 'It's not pregnancy or anything of the sort – the thing is that my voice has become extremely beautiful.'

Abdul Hamid fastened his gaze on her for several seconds, during which he remained at a loss. Then he burst into hysterical laughter, as though he had just heard a joke without an end. Blood gushed to his brain making his puffed-up head look like a red balloon on the point of bursting. His features and teeth went on making agitated movements which were only brought to a halt by the angry voice of his wife.

'Just listen, first.'

He seated himself and she began to recount to him exactly what had happened to her. After he had left for work in the morning, and after the children had gone off to their schools, she had as usual remained alone in the house and had set about her housework: sweeping and dusting and cooking and tidying up the rooms. After the call to the noon prayer she had said to herself, 'Go off, my girl, to the bathroom and pour a pail of water over yourself and you'll feel refreshed and get rid of the dirt.'

It was after Sayyida had taken her clothes off and washed her head a couple of times, and while she was removing the soap from her eyes, that it occurred to her to sing and amuse herself as usual. No sooner had she begun with the song '*I love the life of freedom*' than she felt as though some other person had come into the bathroom with her and had begun to sing in her place. The voice was not her own voice, the one she had become accustomed to; instead it was a beautiful melodious voice wholly unrelated to her own. She immediately splashed some water on to her eyes to get rid of the soap and gazed round the bathroom. She wheeled about in search of a human being or some other creature, while invoking God's name and seeking to be protected from the Devil. But her eyes fell on nothing but the single window, which was firmly closed, the mirror over the basin, with the toothbrushes placed on the shelf, and her clean clothes, which she'd just got out of the cupboard, hanging on the nail on the back of the door. She muttered, 'There is no god but God!' and went on with her shower. When she was sure that there was no sound except that of the water flowing over her body, she continued with her singing of '*I love the life of freedom*'. The voice that issued from her was even more beautiful, clear and strong. The loufa in her hand became as though nailed to her thigh, which she had begun to scrub. She said, 'In the name of God the Merciful, the compassionate,' and, 'I take my refuge in God from the accursed Devil,' and despite her belief that there were no *afreets*, except for human beings themselves, she was nevertheless frightened. Her heart was beating hard and she called out to herself in a low voice: 'Sayyida, Sayyida.' Back came a voice other than that which she knew. It was too beautiful. So she began to raise her voice still further and to put inflections into it, 'O Sayyida . . . O Sayyida,' at the same time overcome by a state of joyous rapture. However, she suddenly came to her senses.

'Perhaps someone had heard me, or you had returned home, Abdul Hamid, for one reason or another, and had heard me calling to myself. You would think I'd gone off my head or was a bit touched. So I kept quiet and terror made of my tongue a piece of dried firewood, while my teeth were chattering, and I said to myself, "Maybe it really is a question of *afreets*." So I began reciting to myself. I said, "I seek refuge in the Lord of the Daybreak from the evil of that which He created", right through till I'd finished the chapter. I dried my body with the towel, and in my confusion I put my *galabia* on back to front. I then opened the door and went running to the window, looking down at the people in the street and feeling less alone. When I was back to my old self and had relaxed, I went and sat on the sofa and did my hair. After that, as though I had heard some disembodied voice calling to me, I found myself once again singing, "*O sweetness of the world, O sweetness.*" Imagine, my dear Abdul Hamid, I found that my voice was even sweeter, a voice that might have issued from Paradise, a magical voice that was unrivalled in this world. To tell you the truth, I was delighted and at peace with myself. The sensation of fear had left my heart, for I felt it was impossible that the voice was that of a *djinn;* it was a human voice, a completely natural voice and yet very different from my old one.'

Then, looking into his eyes with a deep contentment, she said, 'Please, Abdul Hamid, please just listen to me.' And she began to sing.

But Abdul Hamid silenced her with a resolute look. It was as though he hadn't heard anything of what she had said. He then asked her if she had told anyone but himself of the matter. When she confirmed to him that the thing had happened only a few hours ago and that she had not met a soul since he had left in the morning, he heaved a sigh of relief and asked her to forget the whole thing. 'And don't bring the subject up with anyone whatsoever, and especially not with the children.' She was annoyed that he didn't believe her and swore by all that was holy that what she had said had really and truly happened.

The tears gathered in her eyes as she vehemently denied that she'd gone soft in the head.

Abdul Hamid sat on the sofa and asked her to make him a lightly sugared coffee. While she was putting her feet into her slippers and preparing to go, he suddenly felt sorry for her and said, 'Listen, Sayyida. You're over forty and you've got four kids, meaning to say that talking rubbish diminishes your status and makes you a figure of fun in front of the children. And what would the position be if any grown-up person in his senses were to hear you? Just suppose that what you say is true – what does it mean? Are you intending to take up singing, for example? Intending to become a professional singer? By God, what a story!'

He laughed with satisfaction, for he found the matter to be far removed from any of the fears he had had. Then he gave her a playful slap on the bottom and whispered to her, 'After the coffee, come along and we'll stretch out together on the bed.'

For the rest of the day things went on as usual, and Sayyida almost forgot what had happened to her that morning. She continued to carry out the tasks of the second part of the day with her usual enthusiasm: she folded up the washing, took tea round to the children while they were doing their homework, and made herself free for half an hour to watch the television serial. When Abdul Hamid returned from the café, to which he had gone after sunset, she made supper for him with the children, a meal during which he joked with some and rebuked those who needed rebuking.

But in the evening, when she was on her own, Abdul Hamid having gone to sleep, she thought confusedly as to what she really was going to do about her voice, that beautiful voice that she had suddenly discovered was buried inside her, like someone who has come across a wonderful treasure and doesn't know what to do with it. She began actively to think, but always came back to the same logical answer: a beautiful voice is made for singing. So why didn't she sing and let people hear her voice? She was tempted to believe that it was only right that people should hear her voice, and that a person's voice had nothing to do with his age. What was wrong with people listening to someone's voice regardless of age or whether he was a man or a woman? She had more or less become convinced by this line of thought, when she became possessed of an overwhelming desire to sit in bed and sing 'O sweetness of the world, O sweetness'.

So she started to sit down but, just as she was about to open her mouth and begin, Abdul Hamid turned over in bed and became aware of her. He looked at her anxiously and asked, 'What's wrong, Sayyida?'

She said she was on her way to the kitchen for a drink of water because her mouth was a bit dry.

On the following morning, when she began to sing, Sayyida became madly excited. Standing in front of the sink and washing the dishes left over from breakfast after Abdul Hamid and the children had gone out, she again heard that beautiful voice that sounded so fascinating, unearthly and overflowing with power and purity. She was seized with a feeling that she was some other being,

63

with no connection with the Sayyida she knew, the Sayyida that dusted and swept and did her head up in a kerchief each day because she couldn't find the time to put a comb through her hair. She quickly rinsed her hands of soap, drying them with the end of her nightdress, which she hadn't yet taken off, and ran to the mirror. Standing in front of it, she sang, '*I love the life of freedom,*' and her voice rang out anew, strong, pure and clear, like some priceless jewel. She watched herself, her lips dancing with the tuneful words, her eyes sparkling with joyful enthusiasm, her cheeks ruddy with blood which she imagined had gushed from hidden springs in her body, her eyebrows that met and separated in ordered movements, leading the features of the face in a brilliant concord of sounds, as though they were the two skilful hands of the conductor of a superb orchestra.

She felt she was beautiful, perhaps for the first time for quite a long while. This feeling came to her and it rejuvenated her. She stood looking at her face, reproaching herself for the way she had left her eyebrows untrimmed, embarrassed to find a slight moustache under her nose, sorry to have so neglected her hair. Then she felt anger at herself. Why had she let herself go in this way, while possessing within her this beautiful voice? She stood there and came to a decision: 'In order to sing I am obliged to feel beautiful. Yes, by God – obliged.'

Sayyida quickly put on her clothes, for she must go down to the street to buy vegetables and bread before Abdul Hamid and the children returned home. Her mind was still occupied with the same matter, but she naturally had no plan in relation to how she would sing, and where she would begin, and how she would face Abdul Hamid with this decision of hers. She thought of going to some friend of hers to disclose her secret to her, as women do in films, but she discovered, for the first time in her life, that she had not a single friend, no human being with whom she was intimate, nobody close to her heart, apart from her mother and her sister Awatef, both of whom she had at the outset regarded as not being suitable, by reason of her prior knowledge of their attitude were she to tell them of the matter. It would be an attitude of scorn which would have them laughing at what she had to say, turning it into a joke and announcing it in front of any relatives who visited them. She thought of her neighbour, Umm Hasan, but Umm Hasan, despite their very good relationship, had never had any secrets with Sayyida. For the first time in her life she felt resentment towards Abdul Hamid, because he had friends with whom to sit in the café, and there was his bosom friend Ismail, to whom he may have told secrets that he had never divulged to her, despite the fact that she was his intimate companion and had given him four children.

Her state of excitement remained with her even as she entered Isa the grocer's shop to buy some cheese and macaroni and ten eggs. Old Isa had no need to scrutinize her closely to notice that she was distraught. 'Why are you upset, Mrs Sayyida, so early of a morning?' he asked her, but before she answered he had decided that he knew already: life had become hard, and the high cost of living was an unrestrained ghoul who made its way into everything and was completely out of control. Meanwhile people walked about and talked to themselves because of their wretchedness and lack of means (of course, Isa had noticed that she used to talk to herself occasionally). Then he said to her – and he was the old grocer with whom they had been dealing for a long time and with whom

65

they had links of neighbourliness and affection – that he
knew that Abdul Hamid was doing all he possibly could
to provide for the children and that she should be patient
with him. He was none the less astonished when, suddenly, he found her bursting into tears and sobbing like
someone who has lost someone dear to them.

Isa took her by the hand and sat her down in a chair,
then opened a bottle of fizzy lemonade for her, saying,
'Take it easy and put the Devil to shame.' It was morning
and the shop was not yet filled with customers, so the man
whispered to her earnestly, 'Any problem, God forbid,
between you and Abdul Hamid?' It was difficult for her
to explain, so she burst into sobs once again.

When she had recovered, she said, 'Listen, Uncle Isa, I
need to talk to you about something, something slightly
personal, on condition you try to understand me and don't
talk to Abdul Hamid about it, because he's sworn to
divorce me if I don't keep the news well hidden and not
talk to a soul about it.'

Uncle Isa sensed that the matter was indeed grave, and
he was seized by an irresistible desire to hear a family
secret that had to do with one of the inhabitants of the
street; he experienced the pleasure of being about to learn
some new bit of gossip that he would quickly be employing, so he drew up a chair and sat down close to her so
that he might not miss so much as a word.

'It's happened that I've discovered my voice,' she said,
as though divulging a solemn secret, and she began to
relate to him what had happened to her and the words
that had passed between her and Abdul Hamid. The man
did not laugh, or utter so much as a word – as they say
in books. When she had finished her story and said to
him, smiling with embarrassment, that she was ready to
let him hear her beautiful voice, so that he might confirm

for himself the truth of what she had said, he scrutinized her pityingly and replied, 'Drink up the lemonade, Sayyida.'

Without drinking the lemonade, she took up the things she had bought from him and left. When, in the afternoon, Abdul Hamid returned, and while they were having their lunch, he told her that, on his way home, he had bought some matches from the shop of Isa the grocer, and that he was going to the doctor's that evening and that she must accompany him.

When they arrived at the clinic of the psychologist, Sayyida was partly convinced about her husband's idea. He had said that he loved her and that he wanted only her good and that of the children and that psychological illness was like any other illness and that there was nothing to be ashamed about. In fact it was quite curable, but the important thing was to treat it quickly, right at the beginning. Thanks be to God, there was nothing wrong with her, but the story of the voice had perhaps come about through being exhausted with housework, or some hidden problem inside her she wasn't aware of, because the inner part of every human being is a vast bottomless sea, and the spirit's secret is deeply hidden, with the Almighty alone knowing what is in the inmost depths of every human.

'What I am trying to say is that it's difficult for a man to know himself, Sayyida, and medicine has been made for just such difficult circumstances. Also, Sayyida, despite my modest education, I am a believer and profess the unity of God, and I don't believe in the story of djinn and *afreets*, because our Lord has said in the Qur'an: "And we have made between you and them an impregnable barrier." Anyway, my dear, let's have a go. All it means is losing ten pounds from the money which anyway is flying away like so many sparrows out of our control. Maybe, with God's permission, they'll bring a cure and everything will return to normal and you'll be all right. The fact is, this morning you told Isa the grocer, but tomorrow or the day after, against your will, you could tell someone else, or something could happen that would make us a laughing-stock in front of people, and all sorts of things could be said about you, without cause. And I, Sayyida, were it not for my affection for you and for the children, I'd have shut up about the matter and kept quiet, but you know I am fond of you since you are the mother of my children and my life's partner.'

They entered the doctor's office and sat down. The man asking her about her problem seemed to her to be very peevish, grumpy and disturbed, also in a great hurry. So Abdul Hamid started off by telling him the story in brief. But the doctor, rapping the glass top of his desk with his pen, asked him to let her tell it; so Sayyida recounted everything that had happened to her from the very moment she had entered the bath, right up to her conversation with Isa the grocer.

When she had completed all she had to say, noticing that the man had listened to her attentively without any interruption, she asked him, smiling with pleasure because of her feeling that he understood her situation, 'Could I sing you a little song, doctor?'

No sign of interest showed itself on the doctor's features. He looked as though he were accustomed to such things. He didn't smile, he didn't frown, and he made no reply. He merely wrote some words in a foreign language on a piece of paper and gave it to the husband with the words, 'Three pills of the first kind daily, after each meal, and one of the others every evening before she goes to bed.'

Then he turned to Sayyida, saying, 'Keep away from anything that causes you stress, and never allow yourself to be alone. Put on the wireless when you're in the bathroom, eat well, but try to go for walks and lose some weight, because you're too fat. Keep on with the medicine, and when you feel depressed and you're in a bad mood, come along at once to the clinic.' Then he stood up and stretched out his hand to her saying, 'Nice to have met you.'

The others went out as usual next morning and she remained alone in the house. She got up sluggishly, without enthusiasm, to gather up the breakfast dishes. She swallowed the food that was left on the plates, telling herself as usual, 'It's a shame to throw a couple of mouthfuls of beans into the rubbish bin. There's not enough cheese left to make it worthwhile keeping the plate for it.' Then she made herself a glass of tea, which she sipped while nibbling at a pastry that had remained on the table. Feeling she had eaten too much, she got up, dragging her body along, to tidy up the rooms and sweep.

While in the bedroom she came face to face with herself in the mirror. She contemplated herself in her nightgown: a pallid yellowish face, despite its fullness, listless eyes, expressionless features, like those of someone from whom life had absented itself. She pulled herself together and tried to sing 'O sweetness of the world, O sweetness'. She made an effort but no sound came from her. She cleared her throat and tried '*I love the life of freedom*', but in no way would the voice imprisoned in her throat come forth. It was as if it were stoppered by an enormous cork. She cleared her throat again and finally decided to practise scales. She was surprised to hear the old voice, the voice she had known since she had first become aware of life, her own voice, weak and hoarse and devoid of any beauty, clarity or strength. She contemplated herself again. Her face was her face of old, the face she had known in times past. She gave a bitter smile, shaking her head with sorrow, then took up the two boxes of pills to flush them down the lavatory.

8

The Smile of Death

I remained as though nailed to the platform while the strange smile on the face grew fainter and fainter with the gathering speed of the train, the smile I had not seen for a second in the whole ten years, no not even for less than a millionth of a second of time that is not calculated in the simplest unit of time. I imagined I was dreaming: the buildings, the people, the trains and the solitary green plant in its pot on the platform. All had lost their customary existence, and I experienced a sensation I had never felt before, except for that one faraway time when I was to have an operation on my tonsils and was counting up to four after being given the anaesthetic.

I raised my hand, touched the features of my face and asked the time of someone passing in front of me. I was trying to cling on to time and place. The last carriage passed in front of me. The smile that I was seeing for the first time in ten years had shrunk, as had the hand raised in farewell, to a small black spot that was vanishing. Ah, Aunt Umm Samia had departed.

I had known Aunt Umm Samia for about ten years. Her daughter Samia and I had been schoolmates from the beginning of the preparatory-school stage, and as the days went by my loving attachment to her had increased. When I was with her, I don't know why, I would feel myself filled with strength and peace of mind. In the beginning I used to dislike her: her continual laughter would irritate me, and her vicious mockery of everything. Once, in the presence of the other girls, she said I looked like a rabbit and I became angry and cried bitterly. Although she quickly apologized to me, it was without any conviction, and she asked me in astonishment, 'Do such things make you angry? And tearful?'

Samia . . . she had a great sense of humour, and this is what I think always made me like her. She was attractive, with a serious appearance that didn't reveal her personality at all. But when she would begin to talk and her eyebrows would lift, and her long nose stretch out till you'd think it was going to fall into her mouth, when that happened, the way things were seen, in my eyes and those of every-one around her, was changed. She would transform human beings into birds and animals and impart human attributes to animals. She used to make fun of people and of herself and of everything without anyone being able to stand up to her joking – and people wouldn't always laugh. I shall never forget the day the headmistress of the school came into our class in company with the woman inspector. When she asked us about the medicines that were required in the school chemist's shop, Samia as usual was fired with enthusiasm and, looking straight into the teacher's eyes, answered sedately, 'Birth-control pills.'

For an instant silence reigned, but then spontaneous laughter broke out; it started with the inspector and the headmistress and spread out till it reached the teacher standing at the end of the classroom. The inspector went out still laughing, while Samia sat quietly coughing.

Some days after that, when the day's lessons were over, Samia took me by the hand to see her mother. She was in the kitchen, standing looking out of the window, while some gravy was bubbling away in a saucepan on the stove. She turned round on hearing the noise Samia made in announcing my arrival. She surveyed me with a look that ended in the abyss of my eyes.

She did no more than this. Meanwhile Samia was making a great clamour, reminding her of what she had said about me. 'Do you remember last year – that girl who brought me books outside the course and who helped me to cheat in the Arabic language exam but for whom I would have failed? Haven't I spoken to you about her before? Don't you remember?'

From the very first moment I saw her, her mother always used to leave me with a feeling of astonishment, and despite the ten years that passed, I don't think I ever really knew her. This is what she did on that day – and always used to do: she approached and embraced me, and bent down till I was touching the place where her silvery hair showed on her forehead; apart from this I never saw, throughout the ten years, any of her hair, it being always wrapped round in her black headscarf. Then she kissed me lovingly on the cheek and wept.

In winter, in summer, through all the months we would always sit, the three of us, in this fashion: she on the old ottoman placed under the window, her eyes sometimes on the crochet work in her hand, sometimes on the quiet street where seldom anyone passed by, while Samia and I would be on the other side of the room, sitting at the desk. We would be revising our lessons or chatting, Samia making jokes while I laughed. Umm Samia would never speak, would never join in the conversation or even smile at Samia's jokes. Only from time to time would she interrupt our conversation by saying, 'I'll make tea,' or alerting us with, 'Get ready to eat.'

Apart from that I don't remember her ever speaking, and of her hair I only ever saw that glistening silvery part, high up on the middle of her forehead, which looked, under her black headscarf, like a solitary radiant star on a pitch-black night. I remember once long ago I went to Samia because she'd been away from school for a couple of days, and when I knocked at the door, it was she, her mother, who opened it to me. She looked at me with tears falling from her eyes onto my hand which was clasping hers. 'Pussy had three kittens yesterday,' she said.

Ah, I forgot to tell you about Pussy. She was the third member of my friend Samia's family. Her mother had picked her up in the street when she was a little kitten, the day when she was returning from the market. From that day Pussy led a settled life in the house: she had her special dish of food and her own bed. When she was on heat and went absent to satisfy the demands of her body, the whole house would be in a state of anxiety. If she was away unduly long, Umm Samia would go and ask the neighbours about her, and often Samia would make jokes about Pussy's lovers who would stay for days on end in the freezing cold at the bottom of the stairs telling of their love for their adored Pussy.

She used to sit on Aunt Umm Samia's lap under the window. Umm Samia would caress her and stroke her head, and the flirtatious cat would move it about coquettishly; or she would throw her cotton reels to play with or hide them under the chairs and the cat would bring them back.

Once when I had gone to see them, she looked at me when the cat was on her chest. She was hugging and stroking her, and the tears coursed down her cheeks in gratitude as she said, 'Pussy possesses special grace. She diverted the danger from Samia when a pot of boiling tea fell over. If Pussy hadn't been beside her it would certainly have fallen on her and scalded her. Pussy has special grace.'

I gazed at the cat's damp fur. She was shivering with cold and licking her coat with the exasperation of someone whose body has been dirtied.

The sole occasion on which I accompanied my mother to Umm Samia's house was many years ago. Umm Samia had been doing needlework for certain people to help out with her meagre pension. That day my mother wanted to have a sash made, and I was happy that she was going to get to know Umm Samia. When we sat down together on the sofa, my mother began telling her about us – about my father, my brothers and me – while Umm Samia listened in silence, not letting the needle and thread out of her hand and not ceasing to glance at the street from time to time as was her habit. When my mother told her about the sudden death of my father of a heart attack twenty-five years ago, the tiny lines between her eyebrows drew closer and joined up, and her thin lips watered in quick successive movements while the tip of her nose, which exactly resembled Samia's, became flushed, and the tears flowed.

Once I had come to know Samia's house, I don't remember a single feast day when I didn't visit them, whether in summer or winter. It was always in the afternoon. I would put on my new dress and take a small box of feast pastries; on the way I'd buy a packet of chocolate for Samia and a fire-cracker to frighten her with, and off I'd go. When I would see her mother sitting at the window, I'd approach and say, 'Many happy returns of the day, Auntie.' She would answer my greeting as she took me in her arms, and would point admiringly at my new dress and kiss me on the mouth. I still remember the salty taste of her tears on my lips.

I don't wait till I have climbed the stairs but call out directly I enter the small courtyard of the house, 'Samia's passed . . . Samia's passed.' This time, without asking permission, I push open the door which is ajar. I enter and she is standing, her clothes soaking wet, in front of the sink. I stamp my foot and call out, 'We've passed . . . we've passed. Samia's passed.' Hurriedly she dries her hands, wet with soap and water, on her *galabia*. She doesn't smile, doesn't laugh, doesn't speak. The tears that were ready to fall leave her eyes and flow copiously down her cheeks. I say to her quietly, 'Congratulations, Auntie.'

A year ago Samia and I graduated.

She became a teacher in the countryside. She would go to the village and return home twice a week. I became a government employee and would take myself off every morning to the other side of the city and return at midday, and not a day went by without my going to see Aunt Umm Samia. I'd drop in on her and ask her if she wanted anything, and I'd tell her about what happened to me during the day, about the difficulties at work, and sometimes I'd ask permission of my mother to spend the night at her place on those days when Samia was away in her distant school. We'd stay up of an evening and she wouldn't stop her needlework while I read a book or magazine or told her about the prospective bridegrooms who were asking for me in marriage, and about my nephew who had seen Samia once at our place and wanted to marry her – but that she wouldn't agree because he looked like one of those donkeys who pull the garbage carts. I would say that to her and laugh and imagine what he looked like, while she would look at me from time to time and scrutinize me with the tears moistening her eyes, and she would ask of God to grant me success.

I don't think I am able to recount the details. After all, it doesn't matter. And I don't know whether I'm sorry about that or am happy at having forgotten them.

The thing is that the last time I saw Samia was at our place at home. She came to visit my mother who was ill and I was going to buy some things and I went out and left her with my mother. From that moment I never ever saw her again.

The long and short of it is that Samia died in an accident on the road passing through an agricultural area as she was going back to her mother from the school.

Do you know the funeral of crows? I'll tell you about it. When a crow dies all the crows suddenly get together in a great gathering for the burial ceremony. No one knows where such great numbers come from or how they all gather together so quickly, and the way Samia's family and relatives gathered till they filled the house from end to end was just as mysterious.

During all my relationship with Samia I hadn't seen any relatives at all, not even at the feasts, and she never talked to me about anyone except her mother. I don't believe she ever once mentioned her deceased father in front of me. When I learnt of her death and went to her house, half walking, half flying, in a state between belief and disbelief, of being sensible and also of being out of my mind, I was, up to that moment, up to the moment of my seeing Auntie Umm Samia, like someone who has been cast from a high tower and hasn't yet landed on the ground. But when I saw her . . . Ah, when I saw her sitting on the sofa at the window, with no needle and no thread in her hand, without tears on her cheek, I shouted and screamed and beat my head and slapped my cheeks and buried my face in the hem of my dress and began biting it. I felt that the huge amount of pain within me was blocking the air from my chest. I was incapable of speaking, my tongue having stiffened inside my mouth. I was raising my head from time to time, looking at her and wondering if she might say or do something. But she stayed as she was, with the same look on her face she had given me the day I saw her for the first time, a look which seemed to stroke me till it came to rest in my eyes, and with that place where the silver hair lay on the forehead amidst the great depths of blackness. I merely noticed that her hand stiffened as she clung to the arm of the old sofa, while a trickle of warm water seeped out from under the black *galabia* on to the bare part of her legs and flowed into her short black stockings. I became rooted to the spot. Opening my eyes and mouth to the full, I instantly took in the picture of her on the sofa with the women who were wailing all around her, the old square table that the three of us used to eat off solidly in place in the corner, and a man I didn't know, wearing a long *galabia*, standing there propping himself against the door – after which I lost consciousness.

That Samia should die, this is something that makes me feel embarrassed and ashamed.

I used to think that it was I who must die. My feelings towards her were always that she was better than me. By the standard gauge by which people judge us, it was I who won. I was the more beautiful, the richer, and often my mother would be surprised at my affection for her. I used to see everything she had as being better, even their poor, small house, even the clothes that we used to buy together, with the same taste and colours, I would find more beautiful and delicate on her.

I would feel that she was charming and attractive, and I would try to imitate her in the way she had of talking, the movements of her hands and her facial expressions, to such an extent that my elder brother drew my attention to it.

When we would go out together, despite the obvious difference in looks and shape of body, many people would think we were sisters.

Frankly, after that day, the day of her death, I couldn't bear to be in the presence of Aunt Umm Samia. I considered myself, before her, as being responsible for the death of her daughter, and felt that I had cheated her. That was the abiding feeling that developed within me over the period I knew her. Indeed, when Samia used to get weak marks at school, or would spoil something at home, or would be late of an evening, I would feel embarrassed and

ashamed when I faced her mother. This feeling became
so dominant that it made me utterly incapable of being
face to face with her. Since that day I did not go to see
her, not even once.

A month had passed since Samia's death, and I hadn't
once seen her mother in that time. Today my mother
woke me up earlier than usual. Half asleep, I heard her
tell me that Umm Samia was waiting outside and that she
wanted to say goodbye to me before she travelled away.

I was like someone who had a barrel of cold water
poured over him. I jumped up in disbelief and ran out
bare-footed to her.

I threw myself at her. She took me in her arms, wiping
away my tears with the palm of her hand, but herself not
so much as blinking an eyelash.

I insisted on going with her to the station, it having been
decided that she should return to her village to live and
die among her relatives. She had sold her furniture and
had asked her neighbours to take care of Pussy.

She walked along beside me, bearing on her forehead
the place where the silvery hair lay. In her hand she carried
a small leather case containing all she was taking with her
to the country. Along the way we didn't talk; neither she
nor I tried to do so. Despite the crowds and the noise we
were wholly silent. In the cab that took us to the station
she would raise her hand and adjust her headscarf then
again return to looking out of the window at the street
just as she used to look, from her place on the sofa,
through the window. When the cab came to a stop in the
outer courtyard of the station, she suddenly seized my

hand before getting out and stayed clasping it for a time. I stiffened and was unable to move; tears did not assist me.

When the face of a man appeared outside the cab asking the driver to take him somewhere we had to get out. We raised our heavy feet and stepped down on to the ground. We were at a funeral, a very special funeral.

I sat with her for a while in the carriage until the time came for the train to go. Our eyes never met; they soared in the direction of the horizon, where there was nothing. I thought of saying something to her, but I didn't find anything to say.

When the train was on the point of setting off, I got out and stood on the platform, close to where she was, underneath the window. The train began to move. She fixed her headscarf so that nothing showed but that silver patch.

I stood where I was, wanting to cry, to scream, to stop the passers-by and gather them together, to seek protection with them, to run behind the train and prevent it from going. But suddenly – I say suddenly – she surprised me by raising her hand in farewell and opening her lips wide in a strange smile. This changed the lineaments of her face, and I who had known them as I knew my mother's for ten whole years, no longer recognized them as those of my auntie Umm Samia. The increasing speed of the train was binding my feet to the ground; I tried to hold on to the place and the instant, the people who were passing by, the station, but a feeling I shall not forget was enveloping me, the feeling that had begun to steal over me little by little when I had counted up to four after I was given the anaesthetic the day I had the operation on my tonsils.

9

The Monkey Trainer

He opened the door suddenly and sunlight flooded the dark, dusty room that lacked any other opening. The three monkeys immediately jumped around, making a great din, hoping for a beginning to the end of the torment they had lived through the previous night.

The first monkey, whom Sharshar the street entertainer had named Zaqzouq, tried to look pleasant, raising his hand to Sharshar in a gesture that resembled a greeting. Sharshar, who had in the meantime entered by the door, paid not the least attention, perhaps because of his haughty attitude to the monkeys, perhaps by reason of his being preoccupied, together with his wife who had entered after him, with tying up the goat they had brought with them. The goat did not find the three monkeys an intelligible reason for its being there. In any event, when Zaqzouq found no reasonable response from the man standing in front of him, he swallowed the insult and supported his weight with his hand on the floor, as though expecting something.

Marzouq was the second monkey. He looked much like

his companion Zaqzouq, except that his body was less youthful and the features of his face slightly larger. He appeared to be of a docile and gentle nature, because he contented himself with looking at what Sharshar, after taking off his army greatcoat, was doing with the goat. Obviously Marzouq did not know that Sharshar had bought it from the scrap market in Boulak. Marzouq remained silent, not uttering a sound or making any movement to attract attention to himself. He looked as if the whole thing had nothing at all to do with him.

As for the third monkey, Sharshar had, for no known reason, named him Maatouq, perhaps to rhyme with the names of his two companions, or because of some vague feeling that he had which told him that this particular name fitted him best. This monkey, whose looks made him appear serious and exceedingly self-confident, remained squatting where he was. He had a feeling of great annoyance and unbounded disgust at being in this place, so constricted and dark, in which he had had to spend the whole of the previous night after they had brought him from the big rockery at the zoo. He had thus become deprived of the view of the vast sky and prevented from rushing about in a spacious area.

The fact was that Maatouq was a slightly complicated character and would take nothing as it came, unlike his two companions. He was also very much inclined to philosophizing; thus, for example, he had spent the entire journey, from the time Sharshar had taken them from the zoo right up to when he had brought them to this constricted room, talking about the probable reasons why the zoo had handed them over to this person called Sharshar. He had said that Marzouq, who was an elderly monkey, was got rid of because he was persistently quarrelling with the other males on the rockery. As for Zaqzouq, he was still young and maybe Sharshar had paid such a large sum for him that they had been induced to let him go. As for himself, Maatouq, he had no doubt at all but that they had banished him from the zoo because he had incited the monkeys of the rockery to go on strike over having to eat clover every day of the week. The strike had, however, forced the zoo administration to substitute on certain days the fruits and vegetables which previously he had himself seen many of the zoo's employees carrying off with them when they left after work. They even used to hide food which visitors had given to feed to the monkeys of the rockery. This reform was enough to allow the monkeys to live at a suitable standard, no lower than they would have had in the forest.

If we have it in mind to be fair, we should say not that Maatouq was psychologically mixed up but that he was merely a monkey with more experience of life than his two companions, for he was the only one among them who had not been born on the rockery. He had in fact been born in an extensive and spacious forest which skirted the ocean and gave to any monkey, even one who was young and small, the chance of climbing the tallest coconut tree stretching up to the heavens. There, too, he could satisfy himself with looking at the enchanting manifestations of nature, where the waters raged with an azure blueness as yet unsullied by the garbage of modern civilization, and the birds sang with variations on more than one theme, and his soul could scoop up unstintingly from that green crowned as absolute king of all the colours, from which there sprang a thousand and one greens to soothe the soul and enrich the spirit.

And so it was until Maatouq settled on the rockery, to which he was taken with his mother. He never forgot that beautiful, extensive life of which he was robbed, a life suitable for any monkey of sound limb and capable of leaping and running and getting his own food with his two strong hands and pursuing the life he liked.

But Sharshar didn't for one moment think about analysing the personality of any of the three monkeys, for he was an old entertainer with monkeys, unconcerned with anything to do with them other than the task of training them in the quickest possible time and in accordance with the method handed from father to son down through the ages, whereby the man became master of the monkeys and was in control of their capabilities. So it never occurred to Sharshar to speculate about the monkeys or to be concerned about their sufferings, in the same way as he never once wondered about their dreams and their hopes in life. He was preoccupied with the necessity of their perfecting 'The peasant girl kneading the dough', 'The bachelor's sleep', 'The emir's way of walking' and 'The watchman's way of standing' so that he might sell them for a good price to another monkey entertainer, or might personally roam around with one of them, making a living in the streets and markets.

Thus, all that Sharshar did was to tie up the goat, which looked terrified and started away in fright directly it saw the three monkeys shackled in chains in the corner of the room. It had never, throughout its short life, set eyes on any creature from the monkey species. It was perplexed by the fact that it didn't know to what species these fettered animals belonged, animals which looked not unlike the peasants in the village it was from and the people it had seen while passing through the streets of the city when they had brought it to the place where it was later sold to Sharshar.

Sharshar's wife went out, then hastened back into the room carrying a long, thick stick. Zaqzouq, as we said, still being inexperienced, didn't stop showing off. He made a slight movement in an attempt to jump on to the stick and climb up it, thus to exhibit his agility and dexterity as a monkey in the prime of youth. But the chain shackling him prevented him from doing this. However, he felt no sense of frustration at this because Sharshar suddenly let out a shout and, baring his teeth, set about beating the goat violently, while saying to it, 'I tell you – do "The bachelor's sleep" – at once . . .' Instead of the goat imitating the bachelor's sleep, it went on bleating, calling out in that high-pitched voice used by any goat that is being tortured in this fashion without reason. Then it tried to free its feet. When it found no way of doing so, it shrieked even louder in protest.

The three monkeys, crouched in the corner of the room, exchanged questioning looks. Maatouq tried to understand what was going on in front of him, but all the data deposited in the recesses of his memory about the genus of goats from the time when he had lived in the forest told him that they were gentle creatures who were swift of foot and ate grasses and fibres and who gave up their bodies without much of a struggle as tasty morsels to the lions and leopards and other carnivorous beasts of prey of the forest. Finding no acceptable explanation for the piece of theatre being enacted in front of him, he chose to keep silent, concentrating his mind in a fresh attempt at understanding.

The strange thing was that Sharshar, instead of ceasing to beat the goat, which looked as if it was on the point of dropping dead – its voice had become a rattling in its throat, its long red tongue stuck out from between its jaws, froth issued from its mouth and its eyes had clouded over – laid into it even harder.

' "The peasant girl kneading the dough," ' he shouted

fiercely, or I'll drink your blood, you filthy daughter of a billy goat.'

'The goat did not understand the insult, though it did understand this wicked creature who was beating it without reason and who would soon be finishing it off for good. It began to bleat pleadingly in the hope that he might have pity and stop, but in vain. After a while, however, without any apparent reason, he did stop beating the goat. Then he put on his military greatcoat over his *galabia*, adjusted his old tie and quickly took the goat outside, reshutting the door of the room on the monkeys.

On the day following these distressing incidents, the three monkeys were exhausted with thinking about Sharshar's violent behaviour towards the unfortunate goat. Zaqzouq, who knew nothing about goats, suggested that the goat had doubtless snatched a banana from Sharshar's hand after he had peeled it and was about to swallow it. As for Marzouq, who was extremely hungry at the time, not having eaten enough since coming to Sharshar's dingy room, he was in agreement with Zaqzouq's idea, though with a slight alteration, substituting a handful of peanuts for the banana. Maatouq, on the other hand, remained very exasperated at the shallowness of his companions' ideas and the low level of the discussion; he therefore hastened to explode the theory of the bananas and peanuts altogether, pointing out that goats were not in the habit of eating such things.

Sharshar did not leave sufficient time for further speculation on the matter of the goat, however, for suddenly he charged into the room, still wearing the same greatcoat and tie, of which the long end hung down the front of his *galabia*. The monkeys, on seeing it for the first time, had thought that it must be the strap by which other people, stronger and more evil than Sharshar, would secure him. While he was taking off his greatcoat and hanging it on the only nail in the room, which was employed to keep in place a cardboard poster of a smiling blonde woman drinking Coca-Cola, his wife entered with the goat. The spectacle of yesterday was repeated, though with certain minor alterations. After Sharshar had changed his expression and rolled up his sleeves, he began beating the goat. What was new was that, while shouting 'The bachelor's sleep', he stretched out on the floor and lifted up a leg – a leg similar to a great extent to one of the goat's except that the coarse black hair covering it was considerably less thick. Then while resting his head on his two arms folded behind him, he placed one hairy leg on a no less hairy one and repeated to the goat his instructions that it too should do 'The bachelor's sleep', and that if it didn't comply he would give it a taste of such punishment as had never been experienced by man or djinn.

When he came to 'The peasant girl kneading the dough', he imitated the movements of a peasant girl lifting up the dough and drawing it out upwards so that it might absorb the maximum amount of air and swell up. Despite the fact that the goat had often seen peasant women in the village performing this somewhat arduous activity, the poor thing had not imagined that it would itself ever do so. So Sharshar stepped up his savage beating, while calling it all the names under the sun, names taken from his underworld. It was only when it was all but dead that he stopped. He then dragged it out once again, violently shutting the door behind him.

What happened, in short, was that after that the monkeys became frantic at Sharshar's repugnant actions, for which there was no explanation whatsoever. Zaqzouq, as always incapable of controlling his tongue, tried to say something, but Maatouq silenced him with a glance whose meaning was 'Shut up', so that he almost stopped breathing altogether. Marzouq contented himself with saying, 'It appears, chaps, that it's a serious matter.'

On the third day Sharshar came and quickly opened the door. He appeared to be impatient. The hearts of the three monkeys quaked with fear, so that Marzouq, who was in pain because the bewildered Zaqzouq was treading on his tail, chose to remain silent. Stifling his pain, he made no attempt to push his companion away. As for the goat, it was by this time in a state of complete collapse, its eyes staring; it was bleating in distress even before its tormentor's stick touched it. When the torture session began, the stick fell on every part of the wasted body. It was as plain as could be, as plain as the sun itself, for every eye that could see and every ear that could hear, that the goat would in no way be kneading the peasant girl's dough and that it wouldn't be sleeping the sleep of the bachelor. In any event, there then occurred an astonishing and surprising thing which silenced everyone: Sharshar, without warning, took from the side pocket of his *galabia* a sharp knife. He then hurled himself at the goat and slit its throat, while pronouncing the words of the doctrinal formula.

A stream of blood gushed forth from the severed neck, etching small rivulets of blood on the dirt of the floor. The monkeys screamed loudly in terror at the revolting spectacle. Marzouq covered his eyes with his hands so as not to see, while Zaqzouq buried his head in the chest of Maatouq who remained staring fixedly and wondering about this terrible slaughter he had witnessed with his own eyes.

The three monkeys did not sleep a wink the whole night through, so strung up did they remain after Sharshar left the room and closed the door on them, carrying off with him the slaughtered goat. The smell of blood not wholly dried filled their nostrils and diffused terror through their limbs.

The seriousness of the situation became all too plain when Maatouq broached to his two companions a question that was, in effect, like a bomb suddenly exploding. 'What would you say if Sharshar were to come tomorrow and ask us to perform what he was asking of the goat?'

Zaqzouq tried to object to the question from the word go, saying that it was impossible he would ask that of them because they had not done anything to anger him or harm him, and that his relationship with the goat must have contained some such element because of which he had been driven to kill it.

Maatouq smiled sarcastically. He had seen in the forest, a long time ago, sufficient things to permit him to reply to Zaqzouq's words that the prey does not necessarily incite the predator which tears it to pieces. But he preferred, instead of engaging in a trivial argument with Zaqzouq, to take Marzouq's opinion so that the three of them might reach some conclusion in this important matter.

Marzouq cleared his throat and, trying to remain calm, said, 'The fact is that I don't think he'll ask us to do that, for we are, in any case, not goats. In all probability he will return us to the rockery – tomorrow at the latest. But even if Sharshar does ask us to do that, what's the problem? It's an exceedingly easy matter for us to imitate his movements, for it needs no more than some effort and trouble. In any case, I think we should think very carefully before we oppose him and disobey his orders, for he is an unpredictable person and wouldn't hesitate to slaughter us in the same way as he did his goat.

'But just a while ago you said that we were not goats,' Maatouq interrupted him.

Marzouq scratched his small head and his eyes blinked in confusion; then he went on with what he had to say. 'Quite right, but you've seen the knife for yourself. He's also got chains with which to bind us, as you can see. God alone knows what other devices and strategems he has which we are incapable of opposing.'

'And our sharp claws?' enquired Maatouq in disagreement. 'And our pointed fangs? My dear chap, don't we have such things?'

Marzouq did not reply and preferred to remain silent, for in his opinion Maatouq held extreme opinions, was of an unpredictable disposition and never learnt from the past. He had not yet taken in the lesson of being expelled from the rockery and put in solitary confinement in a cage after he had incited the monkeys to go on strike over the matter of eating clover. Thus he, that is to say Marzouq was loth to share his opinion or act on his advice because the wicked Sharshar could kill him and then Maatouq's words would not avail him. One's only got one life.

Maatouq spat on the ground when his two companions turned their faces away and began discussing what they would do after their return to the rockery. Zaqzouq said that he would marry right away and would build up for himself a private harem of females to bear him children and carry on his memory in the world. As for Maazouq, he said that as soon as he got back to the rockery he would thank God for being safe and sound and would kiss the ground, after which he would preserve a low profile and keep out of trouble, avoiding quarrels and battles with any other monkey whatever happened, even if circumstances were to dictate that he eat his morsel of bread with nothing to go with it but a condiment of salt and spices.

Maatouq was the only one who said nothing to himself. He found himself seized with a strong desire to spit once again.

On the last day, Sharshar came with his wife – but of course without the goat. He began his ritual by taking off his greatcoat and baring his teeth. Then he took up the stick in one hand while with the other he dragged Zaqzouq by the chain to the middle of the room and called out in a voice that was full of hope of success, 'Come along – "The bachelor's sleep".'

Zaqzouq looked confused, perhaps because it was the first time he had been forced to undertake a role he didn't know well. Owing to his excessive confusion, he performed instead 'The peasant girl kneading the dough', which earned him two hard blows on the rump.

Sharshar's wife, who was standing watching the young monkey, intervened with the words, 'Take it easy with him, Sharshar – you teach him the pose first.'

Sharshar turned over on his back and took up the pose he called 'The bachelor's sleep'. Zaqzouq quickly, and with great agility, imitated him, which caused the wife to laugh gleefully.

Sharshar was delighted at his wife being so pleased. 'Good lad! Fine – now "The peasant girl kneading the dough".'

The woman bent down slightly and began acting out the procedure of kneading, in such a coquettish way that it was only with difficulty that Zaqzouq restrained himself from jumping on to her back and mounting her instead of imitating the movements of her hands and head. But, for the first time in his life, he showed himself sensible and well-balanced. He put himself in the pose of kneading dough and executed it with such charm that Sharshar ordered him to return once again to his natural position, while the woman exclaimed with great happiness, 'By the Prophet, he's delightful and really cute. Offer him to the circus, Sharshar – they could buy him off you for a really good sum.'

Sharshar's wife took out a banana from the front of her *galabia* and threw part of it to Zaqzouq. He snatched at it unbelievingly, for he hadn't tasted bananas since he had been brought to this place. After this, it became plain that the turn of the two other monkeys had come. Sharshar took Zaqzouq back and tied him up where he had been before, while he scrutinized the other two. For some reason he took Marzouq first.

Marzouq repealed the movements of his companion, though without any obvious agility or skill, maybe because of his being old or through lack of ability. Sharshar's wife commented without enthusiasm on his performance. 'Let him be, Sharshar – you can take him around with you and sell him off to one of the young hawkers.'

It seems that Sharshar had already decided to do just this, because he nodded and said nothing.

Then came Maatouq's turn. Sharshar dragged Maatouq to the middle of the room. The monkey walked unhurriedly, without obvious submission. Sharshar screwed up his narrow eyes in annoyance and shouted loudly. ' "The bachelor's sleep".'

Maatouq made a slight movement of his muzzle, widening it so as to let more air into his chest.

The monkey trainer repeated his command, warningly. ' "The bachelor's sleep" – at once.'

Maatouq again made no reply.

Sharshar, enraged, gave a cough and scratched his head, then changed the command. 'All right, you filthy animal – "The peasant girl kneading the dough".'

Sharshar fixed his eyes on those of the monkey, which themselves appeared fixed and utterly calm. Then he said, 'Look here, you'd better come to your senses. Now, don't give me a hard time. Come along, my pretty one – "The peasant girl kneading the dough", so that you can have yourself a banana.'

But Maatouq, who was not by any standards pretty, squatted down showing his privates and began playing with his toes.

Clouds of anger gathered on Sharshar's face, giving warning of the storm to come. His eyebrows rose in astonishment and disbelief, and his thin lower lip extended, announcing imminent violence. Then he raised high the stick, preparing to direct a blow at Maatouq's rump.

An even greater anger had been gathering in Maatouq's chest, not just at the present course of events but ever since the moment when the goat had been killed and its blood spilled on the ground. So, quite calmly, he raised his hands and fixed his claws and fangs in Sharshar's body. The latter, silenced by the surprise attack, began to fight back and push the monkey away from him while Maatouq went on biting him with all his pent-up rage, intent on his buried dream of returning to his vast, extensive world where lay the blue ocean, the great green forest and the magical world of birds.

It is said that on the day following this strange incident Sharshar was in hospital, Zaqzouq in the circus and Marzouq wandering round the streets begging his food with another monkey man. As for Maatouq, they sent him back to the rockery as being not amenable to training.

There it was said he was spending his time talking with the young monkeys about the splendour and beauty of the forest, which they had never seen, having been born in a world full of rocks.

10

Filching of a Soul

To be exact, it was on the very day that Cairo's Opera House was burnt down that Shakir got married to Samia, his neighbour in the street and his fellow pupil at the co-educational elementary school. Nevertheless, the news of the fire, which he learnt of a matter of hours before the marriage, did not affect any of those who had been invited. Shakir, on the other hand, was slightly upset and was conscious of a certain inner sadness that took away from his joy at this important event in his life. He was really in love with Samia and looked forward to the time when she would be his wife and they would live under the one roof until the last moments of their life together.

Perhaps the reason for Shakir's sadness was that, rather unlike most of the guests at his wedding, he was a lover of culture, a man who derived pleasure from the arts, and had attended various performances at the Opera House itself. This was quite apart from the fact that he had liked the building itself and used to have a feeling of pride when sitting back in its comfortable, velvet-covered seats and when walking along the expensive carpeting, pleasures not previously available to the likes of him, in those days when the building was called 'The Royal Opera House'. His sadness was further increased by the thought that the building had witnessed events and times that had long passed away.

Though Shakir had never been a pessimist, had never believed in fate and chance, he none the less had a secret feeling that remained with him constantly for many a year and extended right up to the present, that there was some link between that event and the way in which his life developed from then on. He knew that his relationship with Samia had continued throughout this period to be a good and loving one, from the very moment she entered his home, which was in fact the home of his widowed mother. Samia had quickly got to know his habits and way of life, a life characterized by tranquillity and orderliness and spent after working hours in such forms of enjoyment as going to the cinema, if a good film happened to be on, or to the theatre when some serious play was being performed by first-class actors. On most evenings, however, reading was Shakir's nightly ritual. This was soon adopted by Samia who, little by little, gave up reading popular magazines and sentimental novels and herself plunged into the vast world of books, with Shakir helping her to be both receptive and critical. Only a few months were to pass before books became, for both of them, their companions during the hours before going to sleep.

During the first phase of the marriage Shakir laid down a plan for the coming years of their life together, on the basis of the likely increase in their salaries, whereby they would, while living comfortably, be able to put aside a part of their income with which to confront any contingency that might arise. They continued to go to the cinema frequently, sometimes more than once a week if they happened to find more than one good film showing. They also saw a number of entertaining plays, and after an evening at the theatre would return home in an expansive mood of contentment. The next morning they would go off to their jobs so happy and relaxed that Samia was able to put up with all the stupidities of the public at the government office she worked in without getting annoyed or nervous. Shakir would generally tell his colleagues at work about the film or play he had seen the evening before, and this would become a subject for general discussion in which even Hasan, the office servant who brought them their beverages, hot or cold, would take part.

On other not-to-be-forgotten evenings Samia would busy herself with watering the flowers and plants she had placed in pots on the balcony, or would play with their cat, when Shakir would surprise her by producing tickets for some concert or ballet group. He would ask her to get dressed quickly because, before the performance, they had to pick up their friend Farid and his fiancée Nagwa. All four of them would then go off to see some folklore troupe or to listen to a visiting group of musicians, after which they would go to some place in the centre of town and, according to what sort of weather it was, drink iced chocolate or hot coffee. At that time Samia used to dress very simply and with the minimum of make-up. Generally she would wear dark trousers and low-heeled shoes and would look extremely attractive, with that sparkle in her eyes and her soft hair done up in a pony-tail that bounced up and down with the abrupt movements of her head, an expression of her open and outgoing personality. In Shakir's eyes these simple traits were everlasting sources of pleasure which, when alone, would make him formulate for himself a simple definition of happiness: a woman by your side who will reciprocate your love and affection, a faithful friend to share the good times and the bad. What else was there? The soul's enjoyment of Samia's charms would pass across the mind to the heart.

As the days passed there grew within Shakir the feeling that this joy and happiness were fading little by little. He would have the sensation that there were mysterious attempts being made to rob him of the beautiful moments in life – though he could not fathom the reason. Whenever this sensation intensified, he would immediately bring to mind the Opera House that had burnt down. Once he quarrelled violently with a taxi driver who insisted the whole way on repeating one hackneyed song after another on his cassette player; he also developed the habit of fiddling with his tie and trying to enlarge the knot whenever he gazed at the vast new buildings that were being put up in the city. As for apprehensions about himself, these began to increase whenever he felt a strange yearning to go to sleep under some leafy tree, something he no longer encountered on his way to work. What made things worse was that the times when he and Samia went out together became few and far between. As for Farid and Nagwa, whole months went by without their meeting up with them or even hearing their voices over the telephone. Because of the difficulty of finding a flat they could afford so that they could get married, Farid was having to work twelve hours a day at two different jobs.

While Shakir could be regarded as intelligent, he had not noticed that many things in his life were slipping away and disappearing: a matter, perhaps, of habits, words and situations. No longer did he buy flowers from the vendors wandering round the streets, and he lost his habit of going for a walk at sunset along the river. Also, the habit of going out to the cinema was substituted, for the two of them, by another habit, that of sitting in front of the television every evening and watching anything and everything. On one occasion when they were watching a film on the small screen Samia said to Shakir, 'Yes, I've seen the same scene in a film long ago. Do you remember?' But at the time Shakir, whose particular cultural interest was the cinema, couldn't remember the film Samia was referring to. Nevertheless the incident stirred up within him beautiful memories of the cinema: the ritual of going out all dressed up, the courteous manner in which the usher guided one to one's seat while the perfume from the women seated in the best seats was wafted throughout the auditorium. Recollecting all that, a feeling of nostalgia would take Shakir far back into the past; he would draw close to Samia and tenderly take her in his arms, while the memory of a kiss they had exchanged long ago when the lights had gone out, made its way to his soul.

At such times he would whisper to her, 'Come on, let's go to the cinema tomorrow.'

But they never did go.

For when tomorrow came and they would be sipping tea after lunch, Samia would open the newspaper and search through it for some possible film among those advertised. She would read out such titles as *Killers' Rendezvous*, *The Bleeding Dragon* and *Den of the Wicked*, and she would throw aside the newspaper and groan, 'Rotten lot of films,' and silence would reign – except for the sound of tea being sipped. Sometimes there would be a film showing that they felt like seeing, and she would say to Shakir, 'Let's go to the nine-o'clock session,' but he would object and suggest they put it off to the following day and rather than wait for the bus at some late hour when they got out go instead to the three-o'clock showing directly after work. At this Samia would give a smile of

101

contented agreement, which all too quickly vanished when Shakir a little later remembered, 'Oh no. The plumber's coming tomorrow at four to fix the new pipe for the bathroom.' At other times the obstacle would not be a prior engagement or commitment – it would just happen that they were at the end of the month.

With the passing of the days, enthusiasm for the cinema faded, just as it did for similar things. 'Ugh! It's cold outside!' 'It doesn't make sense to go out and wait an hour for transport.' 'Is it reasonable – five pounds a ticket for some folklore troupe? They'd be better off putting it on at the Sheraton.' 'A collection of short stories for three pounds! Years ago I used to buy twenty books at the second-hand stalls at Ezbekieh for a couple of pounds.' Shakir missed those bookstalls along the iron fence that enclosed Ezbekieh Gardens; they had been part of his soul, his personal history. He had known the place since he was a young student who hadn't yet graduated, and he would often go there to search around for some low-priced book with which to spend his evening in some other fascinating world. When he had completed his studies and was appointed to a post in the government, he had had to cross by there twice a day, once in the morning and once in the afternoon, as he went to and from his home which lay in a quarter close by the centre of the city.

Though Shakir was still in the prime of youth, all the beautiful things had become altered for him so swiftly: they had become mere memories which made him feel like an old man weighed down with the years. The bookstalls of Ezbekieh were one such memory, and opposite them had been the magnificent white building of the Opera House. As he stood turning over the pages of one of the many books stacked on top of one another, he would be able to see clearly the statue of Ibrahim Pasha astride his horse, and a feeling would take shape that here existed some past, some history that extended beyond time. This was despite the fact that those bookstalls concealed behind them the underworld of Ezbekieh, with its thieves and beggars and pimps, and those lovers without hope who can do nothing but sit on a stone bench and hold hands.

Just as the number of books on view had dwindled, the space now being taken up by vulgar, gaudily coloured pictures, so too the books in Shakir's house decreased in number. Even the newspapers and magazines were affected so that a single newspaper came to be regarded as 'more than enough', while a magazine a week was 'wholly reasonable'. And so, with the passage of time, Shakir joined the ranks of those thousands of readers responsible for the decrease in the sales of newspapers and magazines over recent years; as for his bond with the cinema and theatre, it had become almost severed as he became drawn by strong yet invisible threads to a single small piece of equipment known as the television.

During this period Shakir developed, little by little, a small pot belly. As for Samia, her body coarsened, becoming one single mass without boundaries and contours. When seen in the street she looked like all the other women around her, with dull, dust-coloured hair. After a while she began covering her hair with a small scarf, which was finally converted into a headcloth that covered both her head and neck. When Shakir saw her dressed like this for the first time, with her somewhat large nose taking on its actual dimensions, she explained laughing, 'It's better to wear this rather than throwing good money away having my hair cut and fixed.'

By virtue of the daily advertisements on TV Shakir and Samia did everything possible to acquire a fridge, a gas stove with an oven and four burners, a washing-machine, a mixer and other electrical gadgets – 'indispensable in the modern home' as the advertisements pointed out.

They also carpeted the whole flat. This cost a great deal, but by dint of subtle financial planning and having deductions made from their salaries, also by purchasing on the instalment plan, the successful couple were able to buy a variety of things, and in addition to make structural alterations in their home. It occurred to them that it would be best to close in the balcony with metal-framed glass walls. This meant goodbye to the pots of jasmine and aromatic plants, also to the much-loved cat, because 'who's got the time to look after it and there's no way we can afford to go on feeding it'.

The old curtains were also changed to ones that went with the colouring of the carpet. With all these additional expenses the couple began to feel weighed down by terrible pressures. They didn't know where all their troubles were coming from or why. Sometimes one of them would fly into a rage and they would begin to squabble, but the matter would end in the inevitable peace being made. Life would then continue, lived on the wall-to-wall carpeting, behind the new curtains and with all the gadgets, while they sat in front of the modern houses pictured in the television serials.

11

What Happened to Pussy

Suddenly she was seized by strange, inexplicable sensations. They differed from the feeling she had when she was hungry and would begin mewing in gentle entreaty and rubbing herself against her mistress's legs so that she might be provided with some food; they also differed from that pleasurable feeling that from time to time would steal over her body and take command of it so completely that she had no desire to move or play, preferring to stretch and to yawn till her throat showed; she would then begin giving her fur short random licks, after which she would curl round herself or would put her paws under her head. Ceasing to focus her eyes, she would content herself with opening them ever so slightly so that she might follow what was going on around her, after which the most enjoyable and delightful scenes would be depicted in her head, scenes in which she would find herself catching with great ease a large mouse or swinging back and forth as she clung to the long curtain cord.

These sensations, unknown to her previously, so flooded her body little by little that she became oblivious

of the smell of the paint the lady was applying to her
finger-nails and even of the delicious smell of meat that
was wafted in from the kitchen.

Pussy got up, stretched and arched her back. She
attempted to ignore these sensations and began playing
with the fringe of the carpet, but they were too strong to
be put out of her mind; they were like a pain that wholly
took possession of her. She began nervously licking her
fur and giving little bites to the part of her back that was
the seat of this oppressive feeling. Finding that this availed
nothing, she raised her voice in a scream, twisting about
on the floor and mewing piteously. It was thus that she
spent most of the hours of the days and nights, unable to
sleep, with no interest in playing and no appetite for food.

On the day she left, the large man whom Pussy always
saw sitting in front of the lady at meals and sleeping
alongside her in the bed at night, stood and looked down
at Pussy with displeasure, glowering and uttering loud
noises. Frightened, Pussy stopped rolling about on the
floor and quickly hid herself under one of the chairs,
contenting herself with putting out her head from time to
time and looking stealthily at the vast man, of whom she
had always been frightened, for he used to chase her away
whenever she tried to come near him to play with the thin
black string with which he tied his shoes. The blonde lady
began to shake her head and to gesture at the man. This
made Pussy leave her place under the chair and disappear
into her favourite corner behind the sideboard with the
marble top. She thought of jumping up and touching with
her paws the glistening gold bangles that gave off such a
pleasant jingling sound whenever the lady moved her hand
as she turned away from the huge man and called out to
the girl who was generally at work in the kitchen.

The young girl who used to put down for her a large

plate with meat and a smaller plate with milk, came in from the kitchen, with that coloured thing on her head by which Pussy distinguished her from the others, and began searching for her under the chairs and sofa. When she came across her in her hiding-place, she picked her up gently by the neck. Then, leaving the house, she took her to some faraway place where she left her and returned home.

For three days Pussy stayed in that place, fighting with other cats and being fought over. At the beginning she was scared by the barking of so many dogs and would gaze in astonishment at the enormous piles of stinking rubbish. She would search around for some comfortable place in which to lie down, and it was in vain that she looked for the big and little plates and for the meat and milk to which she was accustomed. Flies swarmed round her by day and mosquitoes by night. The one thing that no longer troubled her were those alarming sensations that had previously shaken her whole body and which were relieved after a large tom had succeeded in mounting her – though not without a long battle during which he lost some of his whiskers.

Then, with the skies roaring and the rain pelting down, she had fled from that place, running about and jumping here and there and sometimes stopping to lick at her soaked fur, though there was little chance of getting down to this with all the people passing along the street with hurried steps. Once she came to a stop in front of a shop from which issued the smell of meat, but when the old man seated at the door waved a long broom at her she fled.

When the rain ceased and shining stars appeared in the sky, she came to a stop. Panting, she looked around her sadly, wanting food, warmth and sleep. Her shadow was thrown on to the pavement by the light of swiftly passing cars. She would lick at her fur and then rest for a while. Then, suddenly, she noticed some rusted iron bars beside her and a broken window that let out a current of warm air. With a single bound she jumped through the window and landed on the bare stone floor of a room.

The pupils of her eyes gleamed as she glanced round the walls covered with numerous coloured pictures and nails that stuck out and on which were hanging faded items of clothing. The few pieces of furniture, decrepit and almost falling apart, were propped against the walls. Pussy stared intensely at a woman who was sitting on the floor surrounded by piles of young children; they were gathered round a low wooden table, dipping their hands into various plates then quickly raising them to their mouths.

The woman was wearing a covering on her head which resembled that worn by the young girl who used to put down a large plate of meat for Pussy and a smaller one with milk in it, though this covering was wholly black.

Surprised and frightened, Pussy had begun to creep forward when a small boy, whose nose was dripping on to his lips, called out to her, 'Puss . . . Puss . . . Puss.' The boy got up and, his eyes laughing with joy, picked her up, her weight causing him to stagger.

She submitted happily, for it had been many days since she had been shown any affection by anyone: no hand had stroked her back or caressed her hand. The only thing that annoyed her was that his fingers were covered in grease and she would have liked to be released so that she might lick herself clean.

When the woman saw her she exclaimed, 'What a sweet cat! Let's keep it here so it can eat the cockroaches and catch the mice' – and she threw her a piece of black bread impregnated with the oil in which the broad beans had been cooking. The cat sniffed at it and drew back in disgust, while the woman continued greedily to swallow down the food.

The little ones bustled around her, wanting to play; one put his hand on her head, another took hold of her tail, while a third started investigating where her teats were. She bore all this grudgingly but ran out of patience when a young child crawling about on his stomach tried to drag her along by her whiskers. At this she raised a threatening paw and hissed at him. Frightened, he withdrew crying.

This caused the man who was sitting on the other side of the room, having taken in a long drag from a water-pipe and expelled a blue cloud of smoke, to exclaim, 'Chase her out – she seems to have rabies.'

The cat turned to run away, while old shoes and empty tins were hurled after her. She darted out as fast as she could by the way she had entered, and once again found herself on the pavement.

The cold whistling wind pierced her painfully to the bone. Hunger and exhaustion caused her to give out an imploring high-pitched mewing, though she had no wish to attract any other cats, for that night she did not have the strength to engage in any quarrels or fights.

Making her way through a dark doorway, she leaped down some steps and came to a stop in front of a broad expanse of flat roof. There was nothing above her but the sky heavy with dark grey clouds. She saw a faint light leaking out from the opening of a door which swung to and fro with the wind.

Pushing it with her paw, she cautiously passed through. There was nothing moving in front of her but the form of a woman who bent down from time to time so that

109

her forehead touched the floor, then, muttering to herself, raised her head.

The cat felt a desire to spring and cling on with her claws to the woollen braid that stuck out from the back of the woman's headscarf and swung with her movements. However, she was even more attracted by an entrancing smell which made her take a deep breath. Quickly she gave a leap on to the broken table where lay a tin of sardines. She inserted her head into it causing it to fall to the floor revealing half of a slim silvery fish. Hungrily she swallowed it, though stopping from time to time to make sure there was no one else thinking of sharing it with her. Having finished off the fish, she began, as best she could, to lick the inside of the tin and to clean up with her rough tongue what had been spilt on the floor. Then she sat about cleaning her black coat till it shone, also her face and tail. She was just preparing to jump on to the bed she had spotted and stretch out between its covers when she opened her eyes wide and became rooted to the spot on finding herself looking straight into the face of the woman who had now finished her prayers and, having taken out a string of beads from the front of her gown, was mumbling to herself. The cat was fascinated by the quick, regular movements of the woman's fingers as she counted off the yellow beads and now had no objection to playing, but the woman was distressed at what had happened to the fish and felt a desire to hit the cat and drive her away. But the night and the darkness, the mutual astonishment and the strange look in the cat's eyes stopped her from doing so. Instead she muttered various devotional formulas. Pussy's dark black fur and her penetrating, unblinking gaze gave her a mysterious sensation of awe that flooded her whole being and caused the green tattoo at the base of her chin to tremble.

The woman uttered the invocation, 'In the name of Allah, the Merciful, the Beneficent', while the cat sat staring at her. Her purring quickly increased in volume. The woman gave a sign of contentment, for perhaps this good-hearted spirit who had assumed the form of a cat and had appeared in front of her when she was at prayer was the soul of her departed son come to visit her.

She pronounced the doctrinal formula aloud, calling out to the cat and patting herself on the thigh. The cat looked all around herself, playing hard to get, as though she had not seen the invitation. However, she soon walked up to the woman, jumping up and settling on her lap, waiting for her to stroke her on the head or caress those places on her chin she wasn't able to clean well.

The woman thought about the pure soul of her son. She was assured that it had been gathered up amongst the best of people, for the cat was reciting her devotions to King David, father of the prophets and master of djinn and animals. The woman was confirmed in her belief, telling herself that had it been an unclean soul it would have come in the body of a dog. As memories of her son came to her, the tears flowed from her eyes. She thought of how she had sacrificed her life in bringing him up. It was now many years since he had left her, and all she could do was to stay on as she was, waiting for his spirit to show itself to her. She thought of talking to him and saying, 'My darling Mohammed, do not be sad because I did not pay you a visit at the Great Feast, but I was ill and could not stir for a whole week. Yet I distributed charity to the poor for the sake of your soul, as I always do.' She also thought of telling him how much she mourned him and bewailed that day he had departed. She was wanting to tell him many things about her life after he had left her, but she was frightened to raise her voice with such words in the presence of the spirit. She lowered her head in reverence as the spirit continued to recite its prayers to King David the prophet.

The cat was irritated by the tears that splashed upon her head, so she began rubbing it on the rough cloth at the front of the woman's gown. At this the woman's feelings were stirred still more as she remembered the tenderness of her deceased son. In distress she whispered under her breath, 'I was yearning for this visit for so long, my son,' and she rubbed the cat's back, who mewed as a request for more attention. Thinking that Pussy might be thirsty, the woman got up and came back with a small dish of water. The cat sniffed at it, looked at it, then extended her tongue towards it to taste it, but backed away in rejection.

The woman thought of locking her in, but she was afraid to do so and she muttered an invocation against the temptations of the Devil. Who would dare to imprison a spirit that was used to wandering around at night? Seating herself on the edge of the bed, she found that the cat had jumped up alongside her. She thought of taking the cat in her arms as in the past she would her one and only son. She began to cry, bemoaning her fate, for she felt lonely and miserable. Meanwhile the cat had gone to sleep beside her, stretched out among the covers, its breathing rising up with comforting warmth.

A feeling of drowsiness began to caress the woman. Her snoring grew louder as she dreamt that her child was in her arms. Meanwhile Pussy, bored with lying down, had jumped to the ground in search of another half of a silvery fish.

12

The Bird and His Cage

What had happened seemed to him to be extremely strange. It made him feel apprehensive and worried as he looked out fearfully at everything around him. He didn't know what would happen to him later, though what gave him some reassurance was the presence of that old woman whose face he'd long become used to. He would see her when she came in the morning and opened the window to let in the fresh air, which would revive his spirits. He would watch her as she came and went in the room, arranging things in their usual places and cleaning what had become dirty, in particular those big things which people who came would sometimes sit on. They would look at him in delight, and the long-haired white cat would sit in front of them, purring as usual and opening and closing its eyes from time to time whenever voices around it were raised.

He never understood why it was that they had given him to this old woman to take away, to carry off from that spacious room in which he had lived. He had learned by heart the contents of that room, especially that thing

113

that hung in front of him on the wall and which never stopped moving and made a tik, tik, tik noise and would give out loud ringing sounds every now and again. The lady with the long black hair would come up and look at him, then would return to busy herself with her belongings, or she would look out of the window and talk with her children, who were playing outside, and would call to them to come back home. No sooner had they arrived in the room than they would go up to him and whistle at him in play, and he would leap about happily and answer them with a long whistle. Then he would start to pick up the seeds they had produced for him.

The old woman who was carrying him was no less apprehensive, for at the beginning she had thought how wonderful it would be to own a beautiful little bird like this one, and she had thus immediately accepted when the lady of the house had offered him to her, together with all the old clothes and the pots and pans and other things she no longer needed because she would be leaving the house and travelling off with her husband and children. But the old woman, having taken him off with her began to think that maybe she had not been sufficiently wise; in fact she had not given the matter any thought at all, and felt that she had been somewhat hasty.

As she carried him across the streets of the high-class quarter of the city on her way to the district in which she lived, the little bird's heart beat violently with terror. Being a bird who had lived in a cage in that house since the moment of his birth right up till this time, he had never seen streets before nor vast high buildings nor a great number of people walking about. And all the while, the terrifying clamour, in which his voice was lost if he tried to whistle a little, never let up.

He had never seen such things before, for even when

the lady would go off with her children, staying away for several days and returning with her complexion slightly reddened to a colour resembling his tail feathers, he would stay on in his place in the spacious room. There he would be visited regularly by the old woman, who would clean his cage and put down seeds and water. What he found most terrifying, during his journey with the old woman, were those dirty, emaciated cats who would look at him with bright, glittering eyes, and would extend their rough red tongues and lick their fur and smack their lips. Never having seen cats of this sort before, he was struck by terror. He imagined the door of his cage opening suddenly for some reason and one of these alley cats coming up and pouncing on him without mercy. This made him yearn for the white cat he had come to know in the spacious room he had previously lived in, for it would come up to the cage and content itself with just looking at him and following his movements as he hopped about or picked up seeds in his beak, without trying to touch him or daring to stretch out its paw.

When they arrived at her house, the old woman thought about the best place to put him. Should she put a nail up beside the window on which to hang the cage? Or should she put him in front of the bed so that she might look at the beautiful sight of him when she awoke? Then she thought of placing him on the old table in the corner of the room which was propped up with bricks to balance it, but she quickly gave up this idea because it would mean her having to find another place for the tins of cooking fat, sugar and tea, and for the dishes and pots and pans placed on it, and for all those other things she usually brought back from the houses in which she worked. Having sat down for a while on the bed to recover from the long climb up the stairs to her small room on the roof, she contemplated selling the bird together with the cage which she had put down in front of her. She proposed to herself that she should show him to her neighbours in the building, also to some of those whom she knew in the street, but when she recollected the conditions under which they lived and the tattered old objects that filled their homes, and their continual complaining of poverty, she discovered it was utterly ridiculous to ask them to buy him.

From his position inside the cage, he looked round the small room with anxious gaze. He was horrified by the faded colour of the walls and the numerous filthy things scattered here and there. That fetid smell that emanated from her, and which he'd breathed in directly he had entered by the door, stayed with him. He immediately felt nostalgic for the happy days he had lived in that old and spacious room. He wished that he might return to it once again and enjoy looking at the beautiful, green creeping plants that climbed its walls and the brightly coloured flowers that the lady with the black hair would sometimes put in a vase on the large table. Remembering all this, he would experience a feeling of deep depression and sadness and would begin pecking at his feathers in agitation, intending to give vent to a long whistle of distress at his miserable state of affairs. However, the old woman got up from her place on the bed and brought him a little water and a little rice, putting them gently down in front of him in the cage. He was slightly reassured, after taking a few sips of the water, having become excessively thirsty by reason of the hot weather and the long time he had been without water on the way there. Then he gave thanks to God that things had not worked out as badly as he had thought.

While preparing his food, the old woman said to herself:

116

It is better for me to let the bird go loose, for my time is very constricted and I've quite enough worries without having to worry about somebody else, for I go out at daybreak and don't return from work till after sunset. The bird requires feeding and cleaning, and my health and strength don't allow me to be continually going up and down. Also, what's the joy in imprisoning a poor dumb bird, who is quite powerless, in a cage a quarter of a metre by a quarter of a metre? I really can't understand why people like to imprison birds. By God, I'll see it free before I go out tomorrow, God willing, and our good Lord will reward me.

When the old woman opened the sole window in the room, which had a wide ledge, the bird, looking at a group of birds passing across the sky chirping, reflected that he had never previously thought about other birds. He used, naturally, to see them from his place in the old spacious room whenever the large window was open, but he had not given thought to the fact that they were not living in cages like himself but were flying about in the sky. When bringing to mind the noisy streets of the city and the alley cats, he said to himself: What miserable birds, exposed to destruction at any time without any cages to protect them; moreover, there is no one to provide them with food. Despite his increasing nostalgia for his former life in the beautiful spacious room, he was very grateful to be still living in a cage, and that this old lady, whom he felt at ease with, was still providing him with food, even though it was only rice and not the lovely crushed wheat with which he used to be fed.

In the morning, when the sun rose, the old woman got up from sleep and put on her clothes preparatory to going out. Before doing so, she opened the cage and took the bird in her hand and placed him on the window ledge.

Then leaving the bird on his own, she smiled to herself and said to him, 'Goodbye.'

The little bird stood on the ledge of the window that had been closed behind him, not knowing where to go or what to do. He felt in fact that a disaster had befallen him for he had nothing in front of him except the vast sky, while below him lay the old, grey-coloured houses. Whenever he looked down at them he was filled with terror by reason of the numerous cats that lay about here and there on the flat roofs under the warm rays of the morning sun. He made attempts at moving his wings slightly and gave a few simple hops as he used to do in the cage. Then he flew off, though without moving far from the window, and quickly returned, alighting on the broad ledge, seized with terror after his limited flight in the air for the first time in his life.

In his fright he began violently pecking at the window in the hope that the old woman would return and open it and carry him into the safety of his cage once again. But no one came and he heard no sound from beyond the window except the echo of his desperate pecking, which hurt his small beak. He therefore gave it up, lamenting the rotten luck which had brought him to this sad state, with nothing above this small ledge but the vast sky and nothing below it but the gloomy houses. He looked around him for some place in which to hide, or some small cage in which to take refuge. Finding nothing but the panorama he had been seeing since placed on the window ledge, he emitted a melancholy, wailing cry, his sole form of consolation during these moments.

As she walked in the city's streets on her way to work, the old woman thought about the little bird. She said to herself: Perhaps he is supremely happy now that I have freed him. She was in fact especially pleased with herself because she had decided to release him quickly and had not given him to one of the neighbours' children, as had occurred to her after she had cooked and was sitting eating. Children play with birds and torture them; in fact in the quarter in which she lived they generally killed them. She had seen them many a time doing this to the birds they got from the trees near the river or which they came across by chance because they'd fallen from their nests. She was delighted to think that she had bestowed life upon that little bird and saved him from certain destruction. Her one misgiving was her contemplation of the long distance he would be forced to cover across the city before he would be able to find a suitable tree on which to alight and adopt as his home, for the quarter in which she lived was almost devoid of trees; in fact the whole city was little by little being stripped of its greenery.

The little bird secretly cursed the old woman a thousand times over. He felt towards her great anger and resentment for having let him go free like this and leaving him alone on the window-ledge without food or drink. The thing that really enraged him was that the lady with the long black hair had abandoned him the previous day with a lack of concern no less than that with which the old woman had abandoned him. The lady, after all, used to love him and would herself often feed him; many were the times she would bring her friends to look at him and they would gaze at his beautifully coloured plumage and play with him, stretching out their fingers to him in his cage, and he would give them gentle pecks with his pointed beak in return. Remembering his beautiful past, he was overcome with a strong desire to weep, while feelings of hunger and thirst began to play a savage tune inside him; he yearned to return to his beautiful white cage which he had got used to and in which he had lived

119

his whole life. He longed for fresh cold water and delicious seeds with which to banish the ghoul snapping at his entrails.

He spent the day in this state, thinking continually about the past and his nostalgia for it, without noticing that the sun had attained its zenith and had then, little by little, inclined down until it had taken its leave and opened its arms to the evening. Only then did the little bird become aware of the many other birds that were soaring in the sky as they returned to their nests in the trees by the river, on the far side of the city. Their joyful chirping grew louder as they covered with their whiteness vast tracks of the horizon at the golden red of dusk. The little bird said to himself: Why do I not try to fly like these many joyful birds who are soaring far off in the sky? He also said to himself: Perhaps, if I were to fly, I might find elsewhere a beautiful white cage filled with food and drink, just like the cage in which I used to live and for which my soul so yearns. Thus he spread out his wings, little by little giving up his delicate body to the power of the gentle breezes of sunset, to bear him tenderly off. And as he beat the air more and more strongly with his wings, there stole into his soul an overwhelming delight, the like of which he had never known before. He felt a new surge of life within him, and he found himself moving his wings and soaring high, high into the sky, until he was far away among the clouds, with the buildings of the city now dwindled in size, enveloped in a watery colour far below him. And he thought about how his life had been spent and wasted, and about the white cage in which he used to live and which now seemed so wholly small and gloomy that it would be impossible for him ever to live in it again.

13

A Short Bus Ride

She typed the last sentence, put a full stop and, having finished, took out the sheet of paper with a deep sigh. She then pushed aside the typewriter to the end of the cold grey surface of the desk. Collecting up the rest of the pages of work she had done that day, she put them away in the large drawer and got ready to leave.

The hands on her watch were almost embracing each other at three-fifteen. Having stayed late a whole quarter of an hour over the official time to write that important letter, she had to gather up her things hastily in order to rush and be at the nursery school on time to collect her younger child.

She quickly did her hair, wiped off the traces of ink and carbon from her hands with a paper handkerchief, tucked her blouse inside her pale-coloured skirt and took up her handbag and hung it over her shoulder. Then, with hurried steps, she made her way to the bus stop.

She crossed the crowded main street, her eyes involuntarily flicking towards the sparkling glass fronts of stores crammed with bales of cloth, shoes and perfumes. She noticed a dress in a bright rose colour. She liked it and stood admiring it for a while. She whispered softly to herself, 'Twenty-five pounds – what a price!' She pursed her lips and sighed, then went on again. When she was forced to come to a stop because of the red traffic lights, a flood of cars of different shapes and colours flowed by. She noticed a small white one, inside it a good-looking young man with his hand around the shoulder of the girl with reddened cheeks who sat beside him. She swallowed and gave a sigh. When the light showed green, she crossed the road and took out a small mirror from her handbag and glanced into it. When she put it back into her bag, the black circles under her eyes were still pictured in her mind.

Once at the bus stop, she pressed up alongside the many people: women, men and young boys. All were worn out; distress showed on their faces. There was hardly a place at the stop for another foot. She stood awaiting the bus. It had a hard time coming to transport her to the beginning of Shubra, where she lived with her older son, who went to a preparatory school, and with her younger boy who attended nursery school and about whom she felt sudden apprehension because she was late. She hoped the bus would come quickly. Despite the apprehension, her spirits rose with joy as she brought him to mind.

A slender girl in white trousers crossed in front of her with coquettish agility. She remembered that she herself would, in a month's time, be thirty-six. She sighed and whispered to herself how hard that was to accept. She contemplated the years of her life that had passed like a dream. She had studied and married and had children and, with the boys growing up, her husband had died. She still dreamt her old dreams and yet . . .

The sun had begun to sting her legs and face, and the

sweat that trickled from her armpits had begun to bother her. She wished she had a car so that she could arrive home quickly, take off her clothes, have a cold shower and lie down on her bed and rest. And she wished for something else, something that had not happened since the death of her husband a year and a half ago.

She felt embarrassed and annoyed with herself, for she should not be thinking in such a manner. And yet she was feeling a real need for that. His having left her was no easy matter, she who had become a woman since her marriage at the age of twenty-four. That thing had continued to happen right up to only three months before his death, regularly, twice a week. In spite of herself, she gave a slight smile – it was in reality a big laugh inside her. Why this regularity?

She felt the strangeness of it, the strangeness of her life, and the strangeness of her marriage to that man who had died. She had not loved him, had not hated him, but she had got used to him. In any case, marriage meant a separate house and children – and that was what she had wanted.

Tears of regret rose to her eyes. Soon she was lost amid the surging movement of people caused by the abrupt arrival of the bus which halted several yards from the stop. She ran with everyone else as fast as she could. As she ran, she asked a person alongside her what number it was. When she was certain it was the bus she wanted, the one to take her to the beginning of Shubra, she strove desperately to get on. Violently she pushed those around her away. She passed through nimbly and placed her foot on the step of the bus, which had begun to move off once again.

She pushed aside an old man with her hand and bored her way through, sundering a young woman from the man who was encircling her with his arm. She shouted at a soldier who trod on her foot with his huge black boots, grinding her teeth with the pain. Trying to seize hold of something so as not to fall with the movement of the bus, which had come to a sudden stop, she caught hold of the nearest thing to her – the shoulder of a thin young man who had been watching her. He turned towards her and addressed her. 'There's more room here.'

She moved quickly, taking up a small space. She heaved a deep sigh of relief. He found difficulty finding a place behind her. Nothing separated them but thin summer garments. She began to adjust her clothing; she gathered up her hair, several strands of which had fallen down as she got on to the bus. She collected it up behind her ears, pressing it back so hard that she touched the young man in the face. At the same time an old man pushed him sharply from behind; despite himself, he was squeezed so tightly against her that he could feel the contours of her soft body and the smoothness of her arm that touched the hair on his chest exposed by the opening of the shirt. He called out in an unnaturally loud voice to the man who had just passed by, 'Take care, man.'

What happened after that was not altogether clear in her mind. The bus was travelling at speed and the stops came and went, while his body made closer and closer contact with her. She could feel his breath blazing hotly against her ears. Despite the heat and the stifling atmosphere of the bus, she did not object to it. Closing her eyes, she took his head to her bosom and her hands ran over his features. She protracted the scene until after she had climaxed. It was to the voice of the conductor, after giving a long blast on his whistle, that she opened her eyes.

'Beginning of Shubra.'

Quickly she turned round behind her, her face ashen with rage. 'You despicable creature!' she screamed.

She quickly extricated herself from the packed bodies, without making out the many comments that were uttered, most of which were directed at her. When she reached the door and her foot was about to step on the pavement she remembered that she should have brought some sort of a sweet for lunch for her younger boy.

14

The Shrine of Atia

The Mother of Horus

One day I was called to go urgently to the office of the editor-in-chief of the magazine on which I was employed. When I entered his luxurious office, which occupied the most spacious rooms of the magazine's premises, I found that the managing editor was also with him. Sunk in a dark leather chair, he was sipping from a cup of coffee, held in his small soft hand that had long aroused in me intense repugnance. Each of the men began giving me an unnaturally warm welcome; this filled me with such misgivings that I felt actual fear of the managing editor when, placing his hand in his pocket, he smiled at me. I imagined him taking out a revolver and firing a bullet at me. I seated myself on a chair beside the editor-in-chief's desk, and learnt, after some formal preambles, that I was to be given a special assignment relating to the shrine of the Lady Atia.

Why should it be I who was chosen to undertake this assignment rather than one of a hundred and fifty other

journalists working on the magazine? I don't know, it was
a strange business and, for me, inexplicable. I am not on
good enough terms with either the editor-in-chief or the
managing editor, or even with the manager of the section
I'm working in, to be chosen for such an extremely important and special subject, as both men described it. Also,
if the subject was a journalist coup, as the two of them
were saying, why should they single me out for it rather
than their many other protégés on the magazine. What
caused me even more surprise was that subjects of this sort
were tackled by more than a single journalist, generally by
two or three at the least. However, despite all these self-
questionings, I nevertheless agreed to undertake this
assignment. In fact I was happy to do so, for it was not
devoid of excitement owing to the unusual nature of the
subject – in that it involved the shrine and the stories that
had grown up around it, more like legends and fairy tales.
But the real excitement, the one that induced me to accept
the project, was that the Society of Antiquities was
involved, having decided to excavate round the shrine. I
was really proud, for I would be undertaking a task that
was both special and unusual. Thus it was that I decided
to proceed with it, realizing that it would be a touchstone
for testing the extent of my ability and competence as an
up-and-coming journalist.

I met up with all the people concerned; I gathered the
material and edited it. During all this time I kept the
managing editor informed of my movements step by step
and received from him comments about the work I was
carrying out. At that time none of those working on the
magazine knew what I was actually doing, including the
chief of the section in which I was employed. And when
the research was almost complete, the magazine
announced to its readers that it had decided to publish an

investigation into the shrine of the Lady Atia. Meanwhile I was putting the finishing touches to the project, in discussion with my dearest husband, the late Ali Faheem.

It is difficult for me to write about what happened after that; or, rather, it is no longer important; or perhaps I believe that it will not be important to anyone but me. But what was important was that the whole piece did not in fact get published after that announcement, not even one single instalment appeared. When I asked the managing editor to return it to me, so that I might read it through, he said that it was lost, that it had disappeared among other topics and articles that had also been mislaid. Then he asked me to forget about the matter completely and not to talk to a soul about it.

Can I forget the subject of the shrine of the Lady Atia? I stood in amazement, asking myself how it could be, as I stared in stupefaction at that man, the managing editor, the man with the round effeminate face and the cruel, cunning look that was not hidden by his permanent smile when speaking. I was able to say nothing, or rather there was no point to any enquiries or comments I might make in relation to that decision, which was in the nature of a final curtain to the last chapters in the history of the shrine of the Lady Atia. As of that moment I too took a decision – that I would never shut my eyes to that subject. In fact, it could be said that I was no longer capable, in any way whatsoever, of ignoring it, for I had lived and worked on an investigation into everything relating to the matter of the shrine of the Lady Atia. For months on end I had thought about it day and night. Also, it was the subject that had opened my eyes to certain strange truths previously unknown to me. Finally, the shrine of the Lady Atia lay behind the most beautiful love story I have lived through, moment by moment and hour by hour. If it had

not been for that research I would not have got to know
that perfect man, silent as the silence of the gods, the good
Osiris – as I used to call him – who was born outside of
time that he might remain as the human conscience for
ever, alive and undying.

I was extremely sad and greatly pained, but now I am
happy and at peace, for I am carrying in my womb Horus
the son of Osiris. Also, I am freed of a worry that was
weighing me down and torturing my soul, for all that I
know about the shrine of the Lady Atia will not now
remain imprisoned in my self and in the unknown, for
here I am publishing it to everyone, to all those interested
in the matter, and I shall tell them all I know about the
shrine, or rather what people have said, and what my
archaeologist husband Ali Faheem has said, and, first and
foremost, what the magazine *al-Sabah* announced it would
reveal in regard to this subject but from doing which, for
some reason, it hastily withdrew. I know that everybody
will become aware of it as soon as they have finished
reading, letter by letter and word by word, what is contained in these pages. I, Izzat Yusif, previously a journalist
on the magazine *al-Sabah*, present this subject to everyone
who is interested, in the light of recordings obtained by
me from those who spoke about the shrine of the Lady
Atia. As for the testimony of the unknown poet, this came
to me by post addressed to my home a short while after
the magazine published the news that it had decided to do
a feature on the shrine. As to how the writer of the letter
knew that it was I who had been entrusted by the magazine with making the investigation, and why he sent this
letter to my home address, I do not, as of this moment,
know. In general, the question of this letter has greatly
perplexed me. In the end, though, I came to some sort of
conclusion about it, for maybe the words in it were by

the well-known poet Mr Khalil Yusif, author of the
famous poem 'Atia in the heart, O eye of mine'. In the
interests of truth, I tried to make contact with him and
talk to him, but he absolutely refused to meet with me or
to be interviewed.

The Lies of *al-Sabah*

Recently the magazine *al-Sabah* interested itself in what
was being published in the press about the intention of
the Society of Antiquities to excavate in the area of the
shrine of the Lady Atia at the Greater Cemetery, and
within the shrine itself; the aim was to uncover an important archaeological find, the date of which has not as yet
been established.

So it was that the magazine undertook overall press
coverage of the matter that had aroused the interest of the
public and of archaeological circles throughout the world,
because observers were expecting, as reported, that this
find would lead to new positive results which would perhaps turn upside down traditional theories relating to
Ancient Egyptian history; also that these results would
perhaps resolve all the arguments about the origin of the
Egyptians, their historical genesis and the exact region
from which they had come to the Nile Valley.

The magazine's intense interest in the subject came
about as a result of what was said about the significance
of this attempt to make a new find, the claim that the find
would provide a conclusive answer to the eternal question,
long broached by Western archaeologists and those who
have found no link joining the past and the present, the
question that asks: Are the present-day Egyptians connected in any way with the people who lived in the Nile

Valley thousands of years ago and who accomplished all those great cultural achievements?

Such questioning has led many into intellectual excesses and fallacious imaginings, and even in many instances, into bare-faced falsehood. Some people have gone so far as to say that the Ancient Egyptians came from another planet whose civilization was several thousands of years ahead of that of the earth, and that, alighting in the Nile Valley, they laid the foundations of the civilization of the great Pharaohs. Others have said that the builders of the Pyramids were wiped out with the passage of time, and that there is no link between the Egyptians now and those who lived on the banks of the glorious Nile five thousand years ago. Was it reasonable to suppose that there could be any link between those who used golden lyres for playing temple hymns and those who are now singing such ridiculous songs? And could these obese women the size of elephants trace their origin to the beautiful Pharaonic women, with their slender figures, wearing diaphanous gowns that showed off the beauty of the Semitic body? Any comparison between the present and the distant past is not feasible, according to the opinions of those making such utterances. Besides, it does not stand to reason.

In view of all this, *al-Sabah* magazine, moved by its love and solicitude for the country, hopes that this new find will act as a gag to the authors of these calumnies that are casting doubt on the origins of our people, and that it will provide manifest proof of our true cultural descent.

However, before beginning to publish this extensive investigation which, because of the scope of the material and its wide-ranging issues, will appear in separate instalments, there are a number of general observations that must be made so that not the slightest ambiguity may be presented to the reader. These observations can be summarized as follows:

There is a great discrepancy – even at this moment – between the personality of the Lady Atia and her religious miracles, and between her origin and lineage.

The shrine of the Lady Atia is of relatively recent construction, also the permission issued by the Ministry of the Interior to hold a yearly festival on her anniversary was given only a matter of a few years ago.

There is an official police record, written a short while ago, relating to her grave having been dug up before the shrine was installed. The act was ascribed to some person or persons unknown, and it was said at the time that the grave had been dug up more than once.

The magazine was unable to obtain a single picture of the Lady Atia during the investigation, despite the fact that the lady – may God sanctify her soul – was known to many people and had, it was said, participated in some public occasions. But the artist Ali Husni made an imaginary portrait of the Lady Atia at the request of the magazine in accordance with evidence presented which related both to her personality and to her physical appearance.

The gravedigger and the attendant at the shrine absolutely refused to speak to the magazine's reporter, though the man is regarded as one of the most important links in the matter. *Al-Sabah* nevertheless succeeded in collecting certain information relating to him, information which can throw light on his actual role. The Society of Antiquities also refused to make any satisfactory detailed statements about the question, contenting itself with a statement similar to that appearing in the news item. This, in pursuance of journalistic integrity and accuracy, we shall publish.

Testimonies

The only son, the one who received the sad news:
My mother, may God have mercy on her soul, was a respectable lady who loved people, she dedicated herself to them, and they loved her and held her in esteem. May God be generous with her in her death in the same way as she herself was generous and liberal in her lifetime. I only knew that she had passed away the moment I arrived at the airport, for they had told me on the telephone, 'Your mother's ill, Fouad, so come quickly.' Yet I felt that her condition was serious, so I booked myself on the first plane to Egypt and luckily I found a seat for the day following the phone call.

At the airport, as soon as I saw Mohammed my cousin and my sister Nadia's husband, I immediately burst out crying, for the news was written in their eyes. I insisted on going directly from the airport to the cemetery. I couldn't wait because my nerves had so completely gone to pieces that I was whimpering and sobbing like a child and I couldn't take hold of myself. The fact is that I had pangs of conscience because I hadn't seen her since I had left the country to work abroad about four years before.

When we reached the cemetery and the gravedigger opened the courtyard to the grave, we were disconcerted to find that the grave was open. It was a great surprise to everyone, and we at once went down to see what had happened. Our feeling was that someone must have stolen the body of the deceased, for this happens a lot these days because of medical students and anatomy dissection. But the strangest thing was that the body was completely intact, and the shroud in a normal state, apart from it having been ripped open, as was the practice in order to avoid it being stolen.

It was the gravedigger who was the first to spot that strange golden thing which looked in shape and form most like a lotus flower, with a single long leg stretched out into the earth. The fact is that this was the second surprise for us. We stood there for a while, overwhelmed because that thing looked so fantastically beautiful. If I had had a *sawwara* at the time I would have photographed it. I say *sawwara* rather than 'camera', because the first word is good Arabic, while the second is a word that has been introduced into our language from outside. It would perhaps be helpful here to make mention of the fact that I am a philologist and that I teach Arabic at European universities. To describe the thing that we saw is now a very difficult matter, but it left a strong and strange sensation within me. When the gravedigger moved in its direction to take hold of it, it made a sound that was like the flapping of the wings of a small bird, after which it vanished completely. I was particularly impressed when the gravedigger attempted to take hold of it by the leg and began to recite the creed and the formula 'There is no strength and no power save in God', while my cousin began to recite the 'Chapter of the Covering' and the 'Chapter of the Resurrection'. What I saw with my very own eyes was also seen by my brother-in-law, my cousin and, of course, the gravedigger, and it caused us all to be apprehensive and immediately to leave the graveyard after relocking it.

I don't know how it was that the news of what had

occurred was passed around but it was, and as a result it became a matter of great concern. It couldn't have been the gravedigger who spread the news because he had agreed with us not to, in deference to the sanctity of the dead and the family's reputation, and because he is distantly related to us. As for my explanation for this happening, and for what occurred later, I would say that there are many things that are possible in this world. I myself am a rationalist and have lived for many years in Europe, and there too phenomena of this sort occur and people are very interested in them and treat them seriously and in a very scientific manner. But we are a backward country, and people here are not on the whole of an adequate cultural level, and thus there occurred what did. My own opinion is that my mother was a thoroughly normal woman, but she was excessively good-hearted, in fact to such an extent that she provoked us her children. She used to show preference to other people in certain instances, and would make presents to them of many things of which we ourselves stood in need. Despite the fact that she taught us and brought us up well, she nevertheless used to do many things at the expense of our interests and comfort. I remember that my sisters would often stay up late at night before the feasts of the Lesser Bairam or the Greater Bairam so as to sew clothes for neighbours and acquaintances without charge. In fact, my mother would sometimes buy cloth from the housekeeping money so that my sisters could make clothes for poor children and orphans. In general my mother was not normal in the way she gave to people, for it was not just a question of being generous. She did it in a manner suggesting that there was some inner compulsion driving her to it. Let us say that she was inclined to be over-magnanimous.

In Europe now they make a study of such cases, assessing to what extent the activity of hormones affects the human body. I believe that my mother may have suffered from an imbalance of hormones in her body, for she would appear sad and depressed when we were not visited by anybody, or when for a time we didn't have any guests, for she enjoyed inviting certain relatives and acquaintances to stay for days or weeks, and in certain instances the period would extend to several long months. It is to be noted that this would happen irrespective of the situation of such people, or their social status, for she used to deal in exactly the same way with people who were lower or higher than herself socially. In any event I can say that my mother was socially unusual, but she was not – God protect us – stupid or incapable of controlling herself, being quite normal in the rest of her behaviour.

As to her relationship with us, she was affectionate and good-hearted, despite the fact that she was not a housewife in the traditional sense, in that she neither cooked well nor tidied up and cleaned the house. This was perhaps due to her having been pampered as a child. I would say, however, that she was careful to bring us up and teach us in the best way possible so that we were able to occupy significant posts and social positions. She made no difference between a boy and a girl in the way she brought us up and taught us. She also gave us freedom in our behaviour and conduct, which would sometimes cost us dear and expose us to criticism, especially when my sisters would return late at night from the cinema or elsewhere, though this did not lessen the love and respect people had for us.

Quite frankly, I can find no acceptable explanation for what happened, and the question of the treasure is one that is in principle open to doubt. I myself cannot have doubts about the gravedigger, because, had he opened the grave after that, the matter would have been brought to light – for we went again on the day following the incident, then on the three Thursdays preceding the ceremonies on the fortieth day after the death, and on the fortieth day itself. As for when the tomb was opened for the second time, it was the gravedigger himself who contacted the police so that they might corroborate the incident. He had entered the courtyard early in the morning to water the cacti that were there, and when he found the grave had been opened he became frightened and ran away to inform the police. As he said to us later, he feared that something would happen before we could get there because letting us know would have required a lot of time by reason of the bad communications. When he returned with the policemen from the station, they didn't then and there go down into the grave but contented themselves with blocking up the grave securely and locking the courtyard. When my sisters and I knew about this we were at first annoyed because we expected him to have inspected the inside of the grave, but it was Uncle Sheikh Saad, our neighbour, who convinced us about the truth of the grave not having been opened again.

Of course no member of our family derives any benefit from what happened; in fact I would say just the opposite, for we are presently afflicted with the question of the burial place being turned into a sanctuary now that people have built a shrine over it and have done what is required to make it the basis of a religious festival and the like. In order to obviate any suspicions, I have absolutely refused, in my capacity as the only son, to have a box for offerings when some wish has been fulfilled, or anything of that sort. On visiting it, it is enough that candles should be lit and the opening chapter of the Qur'an recited. I saw my mother several times after her death in my sleep, in a

number of ordinary dreams. Even were the account of
our neighbour Sheikh Saad's dream to be correct, it was
more appropriate that she should come in dreams to me
or to one of my sisters.

Here I would like to point out that my mother, in
matters of religion, was an ordinary woman who prayed,
fasted, performed her other religious duties and gave alms,
but she had not been on the Pilgrimage because she preferred, when she had put aside a few piastres some years
after the death of my father, to spend the money painting
the flat and doing up the living-room chairs and getting
them re-upholstered, in view of my sister Safa being about
to get married. Not one of us was strict in matters of
religion. Also, my mother had performed no miracles
during her lifetime, as far as my knowledge of her goes.
As for the story of the bier on which she was carried at
her funeral taking to the air and flying, I was not, as I've
said, present at the time, and I am doubtful about its
authenticity. These are the utterances of common folk
who are inclined to exaggerate. As I say, I violently
opposed the question of the shrine at the outset, but I
gave in to the people of the quarter and those inhabiting
the graveyards, and to Sheikh Saad, our neighbour. To
be frank, the basic reason for my complying is due, first
and foremost, to my professional position, in that my
situation is sensitive, as is well known, because of my
having previously been a Communist. It was possible that
this might be brought up again had I refused, because
some people haven't forgotten that I was arrested in a
demonstration in my early youth. I say this frankly so
that the whole position may be understood.

My mother's relationship with my father is something
I cannot go into, by reason of my being the youngest,
exactly twenty years separating me from my eldest sister.

When my father died I was an infant and I don't remember him very well, but according to what I came to know as I grew up and began to be more aware of things, my mother and father got on well together and my father used to call her Professor Atia. But the day of his death was the worst day of my life, because from that time on my mother ceased to breast-feed me, her milk having dried up. She had intended to go on breast-feeding me till I reached the age of six, seeing that I was the sole male child after fourteen childbirths (eight girls and I survive).

There is a small incident which perhaps throws a little light on my mother's personality, being, as it was, one of many such incidents that used to occur at home. I remember it even now because it made a big impression on me. On a certain occasion I was sitting studying in the presence of a teacher of mine who was also our neighbour, and a doctor on the point of graduating from the university. One of my sisters was more or less engaged to this young man. Suddenly I found my mother slapping her across the face for no other reason than that she had herself slapped a young servant boy of the same age as myself for opening the water of the shower on her hair which she'd just done with curling tongs. He had not intended to do it, but she had been leaning over to wash her soapy hands and she had asked him to open the bath tap because the basin tap wasn't working. My mother had said to her angrily, 'If it had been your brother you wouldn't have done it.'

The fact was that my mother used to treat the servants in a very strange way. This boy, for instance, continued to visit her regularly even after he had grown up and become a government official. It was my mother who had herself put him into school and she would also buy clothes for him. She did not require him to do his work as a servant, because she wanted him to be able to study and not to waste his time on household chores. Despite all this, she used to give his mother a wage at the beginning of every month in return for his being with us.

Excavation work will not take place at my mother's grave, for respect and consideration for people's feelings are essential before anything else. None the less, antiquities may be excavated around the tomb, or near to it – that is, in the event of there being any signs indicating the presence of something worthwhile in this area. I would warn those responsible against provoking people; if they don't take my words to heart, they have only to go to the site of the shrine and see for themselves what people are doing at the Festival of the Lady Atia. The shrine of Atia has acquired great renown, and those who love her come from as far away as Aswan and the Sudan. Certain of our relatives in the village have asked that her remains be transported there, so that the village people will not have to undergo the hardships of travelling in order to come here every year, but I have resolutely refused, knowing as I do that behind it are all sorts of aims and ambitions. Some people want to take advantage of the opportunity and make use of it in some way or other, by exploiting the occasion of the festivity. Also, the peace of the dead should not be disturbed, so how do you think you feel when that deceased person is your own mother?

Sheikh Saad:
Our Lord alone knows why I'm speaking out now. I would prefer silence, for these matters should not be the subject of disputatiousness. The fact is that if man wants to believe he will without fail do so. As for the person who wants to have some proof that he can grasp in his

hand and see with his eye and taste with his tongue, he will not believe even if all hell breaks loose, for God Almighty has acknowledged 'God's natural disposition which He has instilled into people'. I speak, not in order to confirm or deny, or to persuade, or to satisfy the burning thirst of some curious observer wanting to search for anecdotes, curiosities and oddities, for I am against the confluence of religion and this world. If this were not so, I would have embarked upon the profession of a religious sheikh and would have sought after the highest positions through occupying myself with the religion of this world. I am, however, satisfied in my life with trading during the day, which does not divert me from the Beloved at night. But what has happened has happened, and Madame Atia has been blessed by God and has become one of His saints. My dream of her is true, whether those who speak against it like it or not. By the grace of God those who love her are so numerous that the shrine was set up by their efforts and not a year had elapsed before there was a sanctuary, a lighthouse to guidance and certainty. And, before everything else, I would tell you that I have known the Lady Atia from father to son, from generation to generation, for it was her grandfather who brought up my father when his own father died, and it was her father who was a peer to my brother in his childhood and youth. And when the Generous One bestowed on him Atia after his wife had had seven males who had died, he gave her this name as a good omen of God's gift,* in compliance with His will after the world had darkened before him, though he bore the matter with patience and did not divorce his wife and marry a second one. Atia – as my mother used to relate, for I was born after her – was an

---

* *Atia* in Arabic means 'gift'.

unusual child in respect of size and growth. This was perhaps due to her having been suckled on donkeys' milk, directly at birth, upon the recommendation of a gypsy woman, a fortune-teller, who had foretold her birth – and God is most knowing.

Atia grew up robust and healthy and much older than her years. It was said that she could carry a sheep weighing twenty pounds – indefatigable and untiring – as a mother would carry her infant child. I recollect that when, in our youth, we would play together 'Eat okra' or 'Kick high', Atia would run so fast she outstripped everyone else, and would jump in a way that those older than her could not. It was said that she was a voracious eater as a child, not satisfied by being suckled, and that she reached puberty before the usual age. At ten years old she looked as if she were fourteen. Atia was brought up like a king's daughter, being spoilt and pampered. She was never separated from her father, who was in raptures over her, particularly about the beauty of her face and the gracefulness of her figure. When it was the time of the uprising around Saad Zaghloul, he would take her along with him and would let her cleave her way through the ranks of those participating in the meetings until she reached the rostrum where she would greet the leaders and kiss them – and then sing. She had studied at foreign schools and was therefore able to sing songs such as '*I am Egyptian . . . I am Egyptian*'. These conferences were also attended by foreigners who were supporters of the Egyptian cause, and thus blood would boil in men's veins and people's ardour would flare up as they saw a young girl singing of the homeland and of its being free. She also used to go around with her father carrying petitions listing the demands of the nation for people to sign.

As for what I have to say about myself, Atia was the

love that opened out for me my childhood and youth, and hers was the heart that stirred mine with its affectionate devotion. But she was never to be mine because I was younger than she was, and it was not long before her late father married her to the father of her children. The wedding ceremony was jam-packed – perhaps this city had never seen the like before. It is enough to say that the celebrations continued uninterrupted for forty days, with every night, at great cost, numbers of sheep, ducks, geese and pigeons being slaughtered, while there were all kinds of sweets made from flour and honey, also rice pudding and the sweet known as *Umm Ali*, and the balls of deep-fried batter dipped in syrup called Cadi's Morsels, and those other sweetmeats known as Zeinab's Fingers, and drinks of rose-water sweetened with sugar. Part of her trousseau consisted of a pestle made of gold and another of silver. No sort of cloth was to be found in her wardrobe apart from pure silk. It was as if her father did not believe he was witnessing the marriage of a live offspring of his who had issued from his loins; being well-off, he sold a lot of his possessions for the sake of this marriage. Thus he spent, for this occasion, on the dancers, drummers and pipers and the providers of flowers and aromatic plants, approximately the price of a house. On her wedding-night, bells were rung and were taken round through the streets of the city, while she rode a beautiful grey horse, with attendants in front of her holding up gauze and cloth, while fire-eaters and jugglers, and men performing shadow-plays, and clowns, preceded them, as was the custom with the people of olden times, until she entered her husband's house, the very same house she was to leave on the day of her death.

However, Atia's father was to die soon after that and before Atia had borne her first son, who was also to die

later. It was said at the time that, when he learnt the news
that the land he was cultivating with tobacco had been
inundated, her father was overcome with grief and had a
stroke, this being at the time of the flooding. He used to
lease this land, which was a large island in the middle of
the Nile, directly from the king's mother, it being one of
her properties. In any event, he didn't leave Atia after his
death with anything other than divine protection and
peace of mind.

I recount all these stories so that everyone may be aware
that I know more about Atia than a brother might know
about his sister, for we were like siblings and lived as
neighbours for many years. So much so that people
thought we were brother and sister, born of one and the
same womb. Would that I had not lived right up to the
day on which she died and had not walked in her funeral
procession and buried her in the ground with my own
hands!

What people don't know – and this is a secret which I
reveal for the first time – is that a short time before her
death Atia came to the wife, who was at the time sitting
and waiting to hear the call to afternoon prayer so as to
pray. We generally leave the door of our house open
throughout the day, because the person entering would
not be a stranger to us, and the wife's movements are
slightly heavy owing to the pain in her joints. Atia was
very disturbed, as the woman – meaning the wife –
remarked. Her face was pallid and she was shivering,
despite the fact that it was summer and the heat was
pressing down on every side. Then she said to the wife,
after she had quietened down a little, that as she was
standing and watering the sweet basil in the garden of her
house she had spotted in the street an old beggar calling
out for charity, so she had hurried round from the garden

144

to the kitchen and had put some meat in a round of bread and gone out to catch up with him and bestow upon him something to keep body and soul together. She found, though, that he had disappeared altogether from the street, as though the ground had split open and swallowed him up. She had searched for him everywhere, but she hadn't found him. Then she had forebodings because it seemed to her that the man had been completely clothed in white; also our street is a cul-de-sac and it was impossible for him to have passed through it to another street, and it wasn't plausible that he had returned along the street since it is fairly long and if he had she would surely have seen him, even in the distance. While Atia and the wife were talking, the muezzin began the call to afternoon prayer and Atia said she was going to pray right away lest her ritual ablution be spoilt, for it was winter and she was often caught short by reason of having diabetes. So she went off with the idea of returning after the afternoon prayer to have a coffee with the wife and to watch a serial on television.

But the divine spark was to be extinguished. We knew when we heard her daughter Sausan call out, 'Hurry quickly, help.' At the time I was on the point of stretching out on the bed to go to sleep. I quickly ran, barefoot because of the state I was in, to their house which abutted on our own. I found the deceased full length on the prayer carpet. Having made her final prostration, she had lost consciousness. Her daughter, who was sitting close by her on the couch, noticed this and ran to call for help. Thanks be to God, the Lord grants death to all. It happened at the time of afternoon prayer, and her face was in the direction of the *kiblah*, also she was in a state of purity by reason of her having made her ablutions, and her intention was good, for she had made the intention to pray.

When I first saw her in the dream, she was reproving me with her glances without speaking. Clothed in a white dress, she looked exceedingly beautiful. I ran towards her, wishing to talk with her, but she entered hastily through an old door embellished with Arabic inscriptions. I began to be preoccupied by this dream and to think about it. At the beginning I would wake up with a start and set about reciting the opening chapter of the Qur'an for her soul. This dream was repeated three times, and on the last occasion I saw her the door had been renewed and was of a wonderful green colour. Then she went through it and closed it behind her, after having waved with her hand and smiled. The next morning it so happened that we went to the cemetery, and I noticed directly on arriving at the door of the courtyard in which she was buried that it was exactly the same door as the first I had seen in the dreams, with the same Arabic inscriptions that had attracted my notice. My body shook and my heart trembled so much that I imagined I must be. giving up the ghost. I felt as though I would fall to the ground. Even my son noticed my unsteadiness and supported me, thinking that I had tripped over the stone threshold of the courtyard, but I remained calm and kept the matter to myself until I could consult those who know about such things, and certain other pious people, and when I did they all said, 'It is incumbent to have a shrine.'

Talking of which, I would say that I know nothing about the story of the golden flower and can find no explanation for it. Such things should not be gone into. Yet every saint has his miracles, and if the time of prophethood and messengers is over with the conclusion of the mission of the Seal of the Prophets and the Lord of Messengers, there have been and will continue to be saints of God in every time and place, because they are the salt of the earth – 'God has created all sorts and kinds', and He alone is the All-knowing.

A final fact remains, and this is that the excavation cannot possibly take place. I say this without any fear at all, because everything that is said about the existence or otherwise of antiquities in the grave is sheer rubbish and has as its object the upsetting of people who would not be able to keep silent were the excavation to occur. Also, why all this running about after trivialities? And what's the point of running after such things? Do they want to know the secret of the cosmos and the essence of life through the grave of Madame Atia? By God, it is something religiously forbidden – forbidden, I say, so have a fear of God in your actions. I would also draw the attention of certain people to the fact that playing around with things interdicted, and most of all the sanctity of the dead, will inevitably rebound on those who so act. Thus the desecrator of graves is cursed, and he who disturbs the repose of the dead is cursed, and we've had quite enough confounding and muddling of minds.

The neighbour:
Madame Atia was my neighbour, sister and beloved friend. I cried the day of her death more than I did on the day my own mother died. She was the acme of honour, of humanity and of compassion. Her kindnesses were for everybody, young and old. She never entered a house without having in her hand something with which to bring pleasure to a child, while on her lips there was always a kind word for the elderly. Those near to her and those far from her, all have a good word for her. As for my relationship with her, I would mention that we lived in the house next door to hers for thirty years. At first I

was a new bride and my husband used to forbid me from having any dealings with the neighbours; we were strangers and didn't know anyone in that neighbourhood where we had taken up residence because of its being near to my husband's work. One night, while he was away on night shift and I was alone in the house with my infant daughter Kawthar, the baby began crying loudly and screaming. At that time I was a young girl with no experience of children, so I attempted to give the child aniseed and cumin, then I tried to put her down to sleep, once on her stomach and then on her back, while all the time she was crying and screaming in such a way that it tore at my heart. I even imagined she was actually dying, so I began crying and wailing because I didn't know what to do any longer, especially as there was not much milk in my breasts, not enough to satisfy the baby. While I was in this state, there was suddenly a knock at the door. I felt frightened and didn't answer, but God came to my aid after a while and made me get up and ask who it was who was knocking at this strange hour of the night. It was her voice that answered me, the voice of Madame Atia, enquiring why the child was crying. I opened the door and let her in, while I asked God to forgive me for disobeying my husband's orders. When she knew, may God have mercy upon her, that my milk had dried up and that the cumin and aniseed had not done anything to satisfy the child, she took her from me and suckled her. At that time she was suckling her daughter Sausan. It was from this time that our relationship as neighbours began, a relationship which was in truth more than that of neighbours.

The deceased was a foster mother to a large number of the children of the neighbourhood, including Ali Abbas, the important person in the government. He, of course, moved out of our quarter directly he obtained his well-known post. She was, in the matter of breast-feeding, quite unusual, being able to suckle two children in addition to her own baby perfectly satisfactorily right up to the moment when they were weaned. She was visibly large-breasted, despite the fact that she was not at all fat at the time of her death. Perhaps this was why children were so relaxed with her and dozed off directly Madame Atia took them up and began rocking them. She used to say about her copious milk that it was a blessing, a favour she had been granted, so why should she not bestow it upon those in need of it. The odd thing is that she used to complain of pains in her breasts when there was still milk in them. She would therefore make the rounds of the people of the quarter and ask who of them had given birth at the same time as herself, so that she might feed their babies with her milk.

Because of this matter of the breast-feeding she was known to many people of importance and influence in the village and those who were originally from this quarter. It was sufficient for someone in need of something, when asking the person responsible in any particular office, to say to him, 'Your mother Atia sends you her greetings, and I am coming from her,' for the man to grant his request – for he couldn't but implement it and accede to her demand lest she meet up with him one day and scold him like a mother scolding her son. Also, some of them used to kiss her hand in front of people, with no fear of attracting any censure. I myself saw a senior officer in the army – there is no point in mentioning his name – who used to live in our quarter many years ago, standing in front of Madame Atia like a failed student in front of his teacher. It was after the war of sixty-seven and she, may God have mercy on her, was scolding and rebuking him,

saying, 'By the Prophet, it's too bad, the country's going
down the drain because of you. The people said it's a step
forward, but you turned the whole thing upside down.
You've ruined it and you're sitting happily on the ruins.'
As she said this the tears were flowing down from her
eyes, while the man stood before her with lowered head,
uttering not a word.

In the days of the Port Said war, Atia stood up for
Surour the Jew whose house lay at the end of the lane.
The young men at that time were intending to kill him
and to set fire to the herbalist shop he owned. She said to
them, 'Surour has done nothing, and what you are going
to do is wrong.' If it hadn't been for that Surour and his
family would shortly have been done for. Nevertheless,
she didn't like Surour and used to say that a believer could
never feel safe from a Jew; also she used to feel great
disgust at eating or drinking anything with him at his
house.

I would say about Madame Atia that she had the title
Hanem because of her father having obtained the title of
Effendi officially from the government. For this reason the
name on her birth certificate was Atia Hanem. Her father
was well-off, but Atia lived the life of the poorest of the
poor and I never once saw her wearing any gold, despite
the fact that she had a lot, and she used to distribute her
silk dresses to the girls of the quarter when they got
married. She had sold most of her gold on various
occasions which had nothing to do with her own personal
needs.

I shall recount to you a matter that concerned me personally. My husband, God rest his soul, used from time
to time to have a deficit in the cash box, for he was the
cashier at the Electricity Company. God knows what was
the cause of that deficit, though – Heaven help us – not a

single piastre of it entered our house. On one occasion,
he was just about to be found out and we didn't even
have anything to sell to cover up the scandal that was
about to break and which would inevitably have led to
my husband being sacked and sent to prison. At this, I
sought out Madame Atia and told her of my secret worry.
No sooner had I done so than she gave me from her
jewellery a pair of gold snake bracelets, making me swear
that I would only return her money to her when things
became easier for me and our bad times were over. I told
her that the pair was too much and that one would be
enough, and I sold the single snake. But God's fate was
too swift to allow us to return to her its value, because
my husband died some months after that – without having
been exposed to any scandal. I myself was then so taken
up with life's difficulties and with having to spend on the
children that I was never able to return the money to
Madame Atia, not right up till this very moment.

I cannot explain all that happened, but saints are people
of miracles, there is no doubt about that, and maybe
their miracles are hidden. I remember that Madame Atia's
hands were a source of good fortune. When it so happened
that she would come and help me in baking bread, the
dough from her hand would yield a lot. Whenever she
stretched out her hand to the large earthenware bowl to
shape the dough into rounds, which I would then spread
out on the pallet and fling into the oven, the dough never
came to an end. Indeed, so endless was it that I would
become fed up and exhausted from sitting in front of the
fire with sweat pouring down in streams over my body.
When she noticed this, she would say, 'Thanks be to God,
it's the last round.' Then she would remove the dough
from the palm of her hand and would make it into a doll.
She would then thrust a straw or something else into it

and say, 'In the eye of the enemy, and in the eye of him who has seen and not said blessings over the beauty of the Prophet. In the eye of the Devilish Tempter' – and she would throw the doll into the middle of the fire.

There are very many stories about the excavations. What I say is that it's all wrong, by God it's all wrong for man to think about something that is not at all correct. It is true that souls leave the body after death, but the decaying body has its sanctity. It's enough that there's godlessness everywhere in the land and that the world's blessings have grown less because of that. Just think of how expensive a loaf of bread has become, just an ordinary loaf of bread, I'm telling you . . . what do you want after that?

The daughter's theory:
My mother was never an ordinary woman. I say that because I knew her in a way that no one else in the world did. The tie between us was not merely that of a mother with her daughter, for we were nearer to being two sisters. Maybe the great similarity there was between us was one of the reasons for this, also perhaps it was because we were so close in age, for I was no more than fifteen years her junior. I was a close friend who was infatuated by her and would share in both her joys and sorrows, and who guarded her closest secrets without fear or embarrassment. I shall be revealing no secret now when I say that the reason for my not having married up to this moment was my mother's attitude. For when I decided to marry it was for no other reason than to stop people looking at me as a spinster. This was about ten years ago when I met one of my colleagues, a dignified and fascinating character who was a widower. I felt that my mother was annoyed

when I opened the subject with her; yes, she was annoyed because I was going to get married. She did not say anything to me in connection with the man himself, but she convinced me in the end that it would be a crazy step which would put an end to my future as a researcher in the natural sciences with ambitions to achieve something in that field.

It was she who had previously urged me to put myself forward on two occasions as a candidate in the elections. I think that she was a political woman, although she had never in the whole of her life worked in politics, except if one regards as political activity her attendance once or twice at political conferences with her father, in the olden days when she was a child. Even after she was married, when my father urged her to participate in women's associations belonging to the party with which he was connected, she went only the once to a women's meeting. She returned fuming with rage at the behaviour of the women and began to imitate them with their histrionic movements. She later told me that what mainly upset her was that the president of the association, a well-known society woman, began to change the tone of her voice and her manner of speaking when some men came into the meeting, and that the other women there began to smile without any reason and to smooth over their hair and dresses. At the time she told my father that they were no more than a bunch of women with nothing to do, and it was perhaps for this reason that my father gave her the name 'Professor Atia' – also perhaps because of her behaviour in general, especially in relation to her private life with him.

Despite the fact that my mother had been blessed with a beautiful face and an excellent figure, she never sought to attract my father with her femininity. Thus, when I grew up and began to understand such matters a little, I was puzzled as to how she had conceived her daughters, for I do not remember her ever sleeping a single night in my father's bed. In spite of this I used to notice that my father loved her, just as she loved and respected him, but each of them did so in his and her special manner. Thus she did not raise objections to his occasional flirtations, some of which she had seen with her own eyes – on several occasions at home with women who were relatives of ours. He also failed in making her into a woman who would be at his beck and call, like most of the wives of her time – in fact of our own time, too. She was a strong personality capable of asserting herself with the greatest of ease. I myself am against my brother's view of her, which holds that there was some defect in her hormones. It was her simplicity and way of dealing with people that made her the most famous personality in the quarter, known by young and old, rich and poor, by Muslim, Christian and even Jew. And I say Jew because my mother succeeded in establishing an excellent relationship with the only Jewish family living in our quarter which didn't emigrate.

My mother used to adopt a very simple philosophy in her dealings with people – though she was perhaps unaware of it – which was to give people the very thing which she herself wanted from them. It was she who was ever the first to give, but she used to get a lot from people without making them feel it. After my father died and we had no income apart from his meagre pension, my mother succeeded in navigating the barque of our considerable family safely to shore, not by managing the household affairs skilfully and economically, but through the philosophy I have mentioned. Thus, when I entered the university – and education at that time was enormously expensive – my mother had gone herself to the rector of the college and met him without my knowing. She had asked him to exempt me from paying the fees – this after a long discussion with him, a discussion that was laced with many lies on her side.

She was in truth an amusing *raconteuse* but her stories and anecdotes were not devoid of a certain exaggeration; sometimes they had not occurred at all, as for instance her saying that she was descended from the Pharaonic kings of Egypt who had become Muslims secretly many years before Islam came to Egypt. She used also to say that she had a book which told of this, written in the language of the Pharaohs, a book which I have naturally not seen. I recollect her telling the personnel manager of a company that my sister Sausan was the daughter of the doorkeeper of a building close to our house and that she had been supporting her small brothers and sisters after the man had been run over by a car. The personnel chief had felt sorry for Sausan and had immediately appointed her to a job. Sausan had got angry when she later got to know of the story from her colleagues and had refused to go to work.

The strange thing is that my mother used occasionally to practise psychological blackmail; thus, through her wide connections with people, she was able to start a rumour in the quarter about so-and-so, the wealthy man who used to share a single egg with his wife for breakfast each morning, and used to store his money in empty jars of cooking butter, and take a bath only once a year. Of course the man wasn't as niggardly as all that, but he used not to pay his alms tax, or refused to give certain of his money away in charity. Many people would protect themselves from my mother's tongue by doing acts that showed them in a good light. Frankly, my mother was a

155

peripatetic charitable organization. Her day's routine was slightly strange. She would wake up early and put our breakfast in front of us; then, no sooner had my father left for work and we for our schools, than she herself would go out. This required no more of her than putting on a black dress and low-heeled shoes and tying a black kerchief round her hair. Having arrived at the front door, she would immediately begin her activity of greeting the neighbours and enquiring how they were – it was enough for there to be a woman at a window hanging out the washing, or a young man going off to his work, for my mother to start up a conversation. She would be able to get to know the news of the whole quarter, just through this short morning stroll during which she would drink several cups of coffee.

This routine also entailed the solving of people's problems: a woman wanting several pounds, which my mother would bring to her during her stroll from another woman by way of a loan; a young girl in need of a beautiful dress which she could wear when she went in with the tray of tea for the bridegroom who had come to ask for her hand. These things she also used to do for our sakes, just as she used to obtain similar services in our name to the account of others, for my mother had participated in arranging many marriages, also cases of divorce, through carrying news and being informed about the daily life of people. Despite this, she was loved, for the final outcome of her conduct was to her benefit. She possessed vast spiritual and physical capabilities, for she would prepare food for a large family in an extremely short time and although she would stay up at night till a late hour, she would still get up early to make the breakfast. She was never surprised at the affairs of people whatever they might be. Forgiving, she would forget an affront and would pardon people their misdeeds; this was perhaps because she herself would sometimes act wrongly towards them. I remember her once meeting a young girl who led her to believe that she was poor and alone without a home or anyone to support her. My mother, fearing that the girl might become corrupted, brought her to be with us at home, having explained to the neighbours and to people generally that she was our father's daughter from another wife and that she had discovered he had married her before his death. The girl remained with us and my mother treated her exactly as she treated us: she would wear our clothes, receive pocket money and help my mother with the household chores, while we set about teaching her to read and write; this when we ourselves were in real financial straits, because at that time we were still studying. After a couple of months this girl collected up all our clothes and belongings, even the clothes hanging out on the line, and decamped. This was while my mother was having her morning stroll and inventing new elaborations to the story about the unfortunate daughter of her husband who had become an orphan when her mother too had died. Several years later my mother met her in the street by chance. After she had hugged and kissed her, she severely rebuked her. The girl wept and said that she had been in a gang and that the gang had threatened to kill her if she did not comply with their orders. She had told them that there was nothing in our house worth stealing, but they had not believed her. She had also expressed the hope that she could remain with us, because she was in love with my brother and planned to marry him.

I cite this story in order to bring out a side of the extraordinary personality of my mother – for she was, in a strange way, reckless in her love of life. She was addicted to cracking open and eating melon seeds and to reading papers and magazines. She would follow football matches and would keep at least one or two dogs in the house; as for cats, there was no limit to the number she had, also birds and tortoises. On one occasion she bought a monkey from a street entertainer who was going around with it begging. She paid a golden earring for it, but it later escaped in accordance, it appeared, with a plot between it and its owner – for she saw the man accompanied by his monkey at the festivities on the anniversary of Sayyida Zeinab, the granddaughter of the Prophet. The monkey shook her by the hand, after itself recognizing her, and the man pretended to know nothing about the matter.

I was very depressed when I went to her grave and found the shrine had been set up, for this whole thing is nonsense. My mother was a woman who has been misunderstood, circumstances having prevented her from pursuing her natural bent. I believe that she suffered from a psychological shock of a certain kind, from the moment of her marriage, and that her life and early upbringing were incompatible with her life after marriage with its traditional demands. She had been brought up to face things with courage and to act without constraint. Her father had raised her as though she were a boy, and he used to take her with him to social meetings of men and to public gatherings. It is said that she began smoking a hubble-bubble from the age of twelve, and I used to see her of an afternoon puffing away with my father with enormous gusto, from the moment I became aware of what life was about. Once she told me that the first shock she received in life was when my father asked her, two days after they were married, to get up and come to bed. At the time she was playing cards with a young maidservant whom her father had given her as part of her trousseau. I cite all this so as to show that my mother was a human being with great potentialities, and yet . . .

The lover and the beloved:
My love for her was that of the sea for its hidden shells, of the bird for the rays of winter's sun that have not yet shone. She was with me every moment of my life. For seventy years her love ran in my blood, the smell of her in my bed at night, her image every morning in my mirror: she was the beautiful dream of sleep, the painful dream of wakefulness. I converse with her without her being with me, I mix her essence with mine, I quarrel with her and leave her, then make it up with her – alone between me and myself. Perhaps they now know, those who asked themselves why I did not marry – I was waiting for her in a way that was hopeless. Time was advancing and defeating us; we were not defeating it. She was not of the same religion as I, so it was impossible that I could be a husband for her. Yet she had been mine ever since there had been love, ever since I had come to make her acquaintance in the house of a friend of her father's and mine. We were struck by Eros's arrows, and they continued to strike at me even in the absence of any hope of seeing her until death: Atia the apple, Atia the meadow abundant with trees, the cooing of doves in the heart, the dancing of moths towards the fire, an everlasting jasmine blossom on my pillow, a drop of morning dew on my window, a sea-wave in my blood. It was she who bestowed on me the face of the lover, the fingertips of him who yearns, the mysterious spirit of poetry, possessor of the insane anthem, of the songs of clouds and rain.

I beg of you, lift your hands from my beloved and let her have her last sleep in peace. What is glory now? Is it a grave with a headstone or a shrine? The earth envelops her now in an eternal embrace that the heart envies, and the beloved jasmine blossom on my pillow is now cushioned by the pebbles of the earth. So bear witness, O wind, and strike violently, O sea, the earth with your waves. O stars of the traveller, pour down your tears as a light of fire, and let the sun set before it rises, for my beloved is being cushioned by the pebbles of the earth.

Atia, whose name means gift, truly lived at a time when gift-making was rare. She did not search for truth, because she herself was it. By the innate nature of genius she knew that good was good, truth truth, beauty beauty.

The only time in which our lips met in that rare moonlit kiss, she said to me, while the river was listening and the breeze mingling her breaths with mine, as light is mixed with fire: 'You are the one and only human being in the world upon whom I would want to bestow my soul and my self. I only wish I could.'

Yet she was able to be beside me for ever, to grant me moments of joy in remembering her when she was absent, and the moment she departed I knew it, even before her daughter came to my dear sister and broke the news to her. At that moment I was walking along the road and all of a sudden her image took shape clearly before my gaze. My footsteps faltered and I fell down for no reason: there was no stone in front of me, no obstruction impeding my progress. I knew that she must have departed on her final journey, and when I recovered from my fall to look at my watch, the time was the very same as that at which, I later learnt, she had departed.

I knew her as well as the forest of trees knows its fruit, and the birds their migration for their deliverance. She was sad to the point of joy, joyful to the point of death. She was the consoler, the condoler, the sorrowful, the remover of cares, the merry. She passionately loved the passion of people for their lives, in flight from a rare angelic love, which is veiled by the circumstances of the world and its imposed conditions that divide and join, bring close and separate: a storm with states of love and passion, and sacred elements of Eros and ardent desire. Maybe I am letting out no secret when I say that my poems and songs were written in the vastnesses of my glorious love for Atia. As for exhuming the grave in search of some relic or the like, I say that the grave is a symbol, a symbol for a heart that lived and gave and took, then went to sleep. I shall not say that it is either wrong or right, for this is a self-evident truth that need not be stated, but I would address what I have to say to those responsible persons in charge of antiquities, and I would ask them whether they have searched in every place throughout the lands of Egypt for the glories of the past, and whether there is no place left other than the grave of Atia? Are you doing all you can to safeguard all the great antiquities that have already been discovered, and is there nothing left for you to do other than to search for some new antiquity? And supposing you did find something new in the grave of the deceased, what would you do with it? Would you make of it a present to every Tom, Dick and Harry of your foreign friends? Would you leave it about to be stolen and plundered and exhibited in all the museums of the whole world?

All I would say is: Fear God in all circumstances and know that your tricks are laid bare. You are only wanting to remove the graves of this area for some reason best known to yourselves, some reason by which you will gain and through which you will ravage the earth.

Umm Husein – an unfortunate woman:
Every single person mourned her when she died, and her
funeral could well have been bigger than that of the king
when he died. She was a real princess who used to send
me here and there on errands and would put money in
my hand from time to time, without anyone being any
the wiser. She knew I was a poor woman and that I had
no man or children around me to run after me and take
care of me. Sheikh Saad was dear to her, also the Lady
Nousa his wife, and they were on excellent terms
together. What the woman who is the owner of the building says about her is a pack of lies. Her daughters are the
very best of girls. The eldest one had suitors coming from
all over the place, but she went on refusing them. I knew
that the deceased was in league with the djinn, for she
used to breed a lot of cats and would talk to them and
listen to what they had to say. Once, with my own eyes,
I saw her giving a large black tom-cat a light blow on the
head, because it was holding between its teeth a sparrow
it had caught in the garden. When she said to it, 'Let it
go or by the Prophet I'll do for you,' it released it at once.
It was just as if the cat understood what she had said, and
the bird flew off. But she went on telling off the cat and
saying to it, 'God's bounty is plentiful and food is thrown
at your feet here and there and you've got mice all over
the place, so did you just have to have yourself a sparrow?'
The cat went on rubbing itself against her legs, mewing in
a weak voice, full of meekness and entreaty, like someone
owning up to a mistake he's made.

Sheikh Saad knew everything about her, and I myself
believed him when he told about her miracles, because I
saw with my own eyes some of the things she did, as I
have said. Also she said a good word for me with the lady
who is the director of the old people's home so I could

go and live there, because I was finding it a bit hard getting about on my two legs. But I found living in the home boring and their treatment harsh, so I went back to her a second time and told her I needed to be here in the quarter, because I'd got used to it and to the people in it. So she put in a word for me with the owner of the large building and he gave me a place under the stairs in which to spend the night, and what with a morsel from here and a morsel from there, things are going fine. She also made me an allowance every month and caused kind people to do their bit by me, thanks be to God.

On the day of her funeral I was as light as a feather, and my foot as strong as that of a mule, so much so that I went with the funeral procession right up to the mosque. I had already been in charge of her being washed. Her body was as clean as could be, and there was light coming from her face. There was a sweet smile on her lips, and anyone seeing her would have thought she was asleep, immersed in some beautiful dream. I took her clothes for the blessing they would bring, and I asked the children to let me have a tortoise which they had had in the house for around thirty years, and it's still with me.

Every other year the government makes a fuss over something. When I was in the village a long time ago, it kept on about 'Antiquities, antiquities'. But people in olden times were clever and anyone who happened to see something here or there would keep quiet about it. The gravedigger, may his tongue be cut out, was possibly the person who informed the government, and if the government were to take the land, it is to be presumed that it would build houses on it, so there's no point in spending the money on a lot of nonsense.

The Wiles of Men

The wife of the owner of the large building in the quarter and of other buildings:

While what I am going to say should not be said about someone who has died, it being proper only to say words of mercy over them, yet it must be said. It is a testimony and I must be honest in it. My opinion is that Atia was in no way an honourable woman, for her conduct was vulgar and common. She used to make friends with all and sundry, and down-and-outs and low-class types used to go to her house and she would spend the evening in conversation, giving and taking with them. She was not a housewife in any way whatsoever, for the food she cooked wasn't fit for human consumption, or even for animals. Her house was always dirty owing to all the people coming and going, and I don't think she ever combed her hair. She used to dress in black and put a black kerchief round her head, not for reasons of decorum or modesty, or as an expression of mourning for her husband, as she claimed, but because black is a colour which doesn't show up dirt and you can't make out how it's been cut, as all black clothes look the same. I completely broke with her, although I was extremely careful with her during the time the relationship continued – that is ever since her middle daughter tried to seduce my officer son. Her daughters all take after her and are good at sweet talk and smiling so that young men will fall into their snares. But they are soon exposed, for they mostly take after their mother, being prodigal like her and not ashamed of being poor or of begging. Thus the eldest daughter went to the university on most days dressed in my daughter's clothes, she being about the same age. The odd thing is that Atia was not originally poor, but she was a spendthrift. When she married she owned twenty-four mattresses and twenty cotton bedspreads, which were

164

worth a lot of money, even in the days when things were cheap. And yet there is not a single one of those bedspreads in her house now because she used to lend people everything from her house, even the mattresses. When guests from the village used to come and stay with her neighbour, she would give her mattresses and bedspreads, and even crockery and knives and forks. Naturally it was impossible for me to accept that my son should marry one of her daughters, who all used to receive young men at home and would engage in conversation with them, and in fact used sometimes to go out with them to the cinema. Is this something one can accept? Can anyone imagine such a thing? Her eldest daughter used to go on trips with the university and would be away for a week or two – and God knows where she was in actual fact. As for Atia herself, her behaviour could not but be proper, for she basically could not be regarded as being a woman that men would look at. Her own husband used to make fun of her about that in front of us, and in front of everyone. As for my husband sometimes joking with her and inviting her for a cup of coffee, this meant nothing, for my husband is a man who really understands the world and used to do that because she was acquainted with the news of the whole quarter and was always the first to have such news. Of course he used to make her loans from time to time and would excuse her with the words: 'Poor woman, she's got a lot on her plate.'

The story of the shrine is of course nonsense. Her neighbour, Sheikh Saad, is behind it, and he's a man who's crazy and also open to suspicion. He exploits his influence over people as a preacher in the mosque of the district. I would say frankly that there must be people who are benefiting from this business. These things happen, and increasingly so in this country. The simplest thing one can say is that she was not veiled in the real meaning of being veiled; likewise her daughters were very far from being properly veiled. Also, is it reasonable that miracles should suddenly occur? By God, I am astonished by that, and even more astonished by the interest shown by the press in things of this sort. Thus I am drawing your attention to what is occurring in the country now: the immorality of the tenants and the way in which they play fast and loose with the landlords. I would hope that the newspapers would write about that, for they are even refusing to pay the money for the water, to say nothing of the rents themselves being low. In this connection I would mention that Atia once sent a letter of thanks in the name of the inhabitants of the quarter to a late President of the Republic who had made a general lowering of rents long years ago. Behind every way of behaving there is some advantage to someone, so the government should search out the people who will benefit from the business of Atia. My object from these words is clear, and those who understand these things more than I do are well aware of it.

A university student among those who carried it:
We left with the bier from the house and walked with it to the mosque in order to perform the funeral prayer. The distance was about two kilometres. It was wintertime, but the weather was reasonably good and the sun was shining. Suddenly, as we were going along, and without any warning, it became cloudy and began pouring with rain. At that moment something strange began to happen, for the bier started to get lighter and to slip from our hands, darting off at great speed to the mosque. We went on hanging on to it and trying to steady it, while running at

its speed so that it wouldn't slip from our grasp and fall into the mud. All of those who were carrying it with me felt the same thing, and there were five persons besides myself. I didn't believe it to begin with, and I thought I was imagining what I'm saying, until the rest of the six people repeated it among themselves. There is something further, and that is that we heard, while placing the bier on the ground at the mosque for the prayer, an unusual creaking of bones. I say this now, hoping that those who do not believe in such things will believe me, because I used to be like them, not thinking that stories of this sort really do happen. I have spent a lot of time thinking about that incident before arriving at a definite conclusion about it. I can explain this occurrence, and many other matters, on the strength of data provided by ancient Egyptian history. Thus the goddess of justice, Maat, enacts the placing of the heart of the deceased in a balance and weighs it so that its fate may be determined. If the heart is heavy owing to the many sins and wrongs it bears, it goes to the Fire, and if it is light and clean its owner will have the good fortune to go to Heaven. From this it is possible to imagine that the bier began to fly perhaps at the very moment when the truth about the heart of its owner was made known and the divine decision was taken in relation to its going to Heaven. All the premises lead to this conclusion, for the Lady Atia was famed for generosity and for having a natural propensity for doing good; she was also famed for her many favours to all the people of the quarter, favours that were countless, and she was sweet-spoken and kindly in her behaviour and speech. All this makes her scale of the balance in the Hereafter incline towards the direction of entering Heaven. She may well have had manifestations and miracles that were hidden from the world, as the Sufis say.

The question of the Lady Atia has occupied me greatly, as I have said. On investigating the accompanying circumstances of all the stories and incidents, I have reached a conclusion of the utmost importance: this is that the Lady Atia used to belong to the race of the great Akhenaton without her knowing it, and that she carried within her the spirit of the ancient teachings of Akhenaton about the unconscious. Through research I have discovered that she came from the same district in which the teachings of Akhenaton thrived and flourished, the area from which emanated every idea inviting the sacrifice of self to the love of the One Creator, the Origin of Existence. I attempted to trace the path of the teachings of Akhenaton historically and to join up those threads that had been severed along the way and which could guide us to the state at which these teachings had reached. It is not acceptable, either in reason or logic, that these lofty teachings should suddenly have declined at that time merely because of newly created political issues. I am able to say that the teachings continued to exercise their influence up to our present time, after they had seeped through into numerous different intellectual channels. Perhaps the most outstanding manifestations of this influence is what is now being raised about the question of the Lady Atia. The idea of Sufism is an idea originating with Akhenaton, summarized in withdrawal from the world and in worship and yearning so that the lover becomes one with the beloved.

Here I would like to turn my attention to what is contained in the books of the historians of the Middle Period about Akhenaton, for King Surid, in the language of those chroniclers, who was himself Akhenaton, used to cross the Nile, he and his three daughters, and leave his capital. He would go through a secret tunnel and make his way to the other shore of the river where lay the vast extended desert and the golden captivating sun, to practise the with-drawal from the world to which I have referred. It was the same method which was later followed by the Abba Bakhoum, the founder of monasticism in Egypt and the entire world. Then there was also the famous Egyptian Sufi, al-Niffari, who followed the same method. I think that he was also Saint Abba Nafar, the monastic monk, specially as the personality of al-Niffari is surrounded by a great deal of vagueness about matters such as his place of origin and his way of life, even though the question of his having withdrawn from life in order to worship in the desert is wholly settled as to its authenticity. It is to be remarked that most of the Muslim Sufis came from Upper Egypt, and in fact some of them were acquainted with the Ancient Egyptian language. Thus of Dhu l-Nun, who was of Aswani origin, it is recounted, according to the writings of the Middle Period, that he used to read what was written on the ancient temples that were spread along the banks of the Nile, by which was meant the numerous Pharaonic antiquities to be found in Upper Egypt. Fur-thermore, there is a great similarity between the utterances of al-Niffari and those of Akhenaton.

Perhaps that has been the subject of some long piece of research, but I have presented all these words in an attempt to arrive at a part of the truth in the matter of the Lady Atia. I do not support, in a general way, what happened, neither do I reject it categorically on a scientific and materialistic basis. I would ask that everybody should hurry up with the excavation operations, there being no point in impeding matters, particularly after what was seen by her son and the gravedigger. This story is an important indicator of the relationship I have mentioned between the beliefs of Akhenaton and the Lady Atia, and I believe the time has now come for us to be in touch

with everything that is secret and invisible in a scientific
and studied manner and that we should give a little free
rein for the truths of history to speak out. Finally, I would
like to say, to those who fear for the shrine of the Lady
Atia, that excavations would perhaps replace doubt with
certainty and increase the worth and standing of the shrine
of the Lady Atia, and would in fact bring profit and benefit
to all.

Awwad the silent:
Awwad the gravedigger refused, as *al-Sabah* previously
reported, to provide the magazine with any information
– he being the gravedigger in charge of looking after and
attending to the shrine of the Lady Atia. The courtyard
of the cemetery in which the shrine lies is also within the
area of his authority. Nevertheless *al-Sabah* was able to
obtain information relating to Awwad the gravedigger,
and maybe this information throws some light on his
personality and his activity in the district.

M.A., the reciter of the Qur'an over the graves in the
cemetery, says: 'Awwad is the first person to benefit from
what is happening now, because he is the sole person
who can know when and why and how the grave was
desecrated. My opinion is that the whole story is his
invention. As for the information I would like to com-
municate to the government and those responsible – it is
that Awwad sells the corpses to medical students. That is
something that cannot be kept quiet about. I myself possess full information about the matter, details of prices
and a lot of other matters which will be of great use to
the government.'

S. F., gravedigger at the cemetery, says: 'Awwad is by nature a thief who's turned over a new leaf. He came to this district ages ago, because the government was after him, then landed up in the cemetery and worked as a gravedigger. He knows all about the tombs, brick by brick and stone by stone. If there had ever been treasure, then he would have stolen it a long time ago and would have become rich and left the graveyard and its lugubrious life. My opinion is that he is not a man to benefit from the whole business in any way whatsoever. As regards the shrine of the Lady Atia, it is new and no one knows it well, which means that the income from it is limited. Also, had he stolen anything from the grave, that is to say gold or something of the sort, he would surely have filled it up again with earth so that he would not be found out. And he himself, the night of the incident, was extremely perplexed and disturbed, and he came to me to the house and related the story to me. Of course he refused to talk about anything because such matters are sensitive from many viewpoints and they should not be discussed.

The archaeologist, Ali Faheem:
I shall talk, despite my conviction that such talk is useless, for I doubt whether my words will be published at all. For my words are altogether unsuitable for publication in a magazine such as *al-Sabah*, and perhaps unsuitable to appear in any other publication that is issued and distributed to the public during this period of time. For everything that is said about the freedom of the press and the freedom of expression is a big lie that I have not believed in and will not believe in so long as I live. Yet, anyhow, I shall consider that I am speaking to myself, as the habit is. The difference is that here I shall be speaking to myself

in a slightly louder voice, this perhaps being a simple attempt to escape from madness, which I feel approaching me with terrifying speed. I am no longer able to bear the superabundance of lying and falsehood that has come to affect everything and which envelops everything in our life from the tips of our toes to the tops of our heads.

I have arranged my retirement from archaeology, despite my having many long years ahead of me during which I would, from the legal point of view, be allowed to continue working. I strove to effect a quiet withdrawal when I felt that everything had got completely out of hand. It became no longer possible for me to bear it or to perform a role counter to the wilful and deliberate sabotage that was occurring. The matter had gone beyond the bounds of negligence, ignorance and indifference to our great archaeological inheritance, for it now affects what is more extensive than that and more dangerous for our past, our present and our future, and for the consciousness of coming generations.

Before dealing with the question of the shrine of the Lady Atia, I would like to state a general truth that I feel, and that is that our country is one that has been ill-fated over the centuries. It resembles a beautiful woman whose beauty has harmed her through the ambitious designs of others against her. The special characteristics of this country have been an affliction to its people throughout history. What did we derive from the building of the Pyramids except death and misery? What glory did we obtain from those vast stone structures that we built with blood and tears? And what did we gain from digging the Suez Canal? How many channels of blood were filled with the sweat of thousands of the sons of this homeland so that English and French ships might pass through it, then later American ships? There is not any feat we have accomplished without it having been an affliction for us, even the Nile is an eternal curse that has been imposed upon us: it is a drama, or rather a historical tragedy that has been foreordained against its heroes, from the sons of this country; a tragedy that has to be swallowed down for evermore.

I say this in order that I may thereby enter into the subject of the shrine of the Lady Atia, for it is known that the area of the shrine is one of the richest archaeological sites in the country. Both archaeologists and historians realize the exact importance and standing of this area from the archaeological point of view, in the same way as they know in advance the importance of the results the excavations here may well reveal. I shall not be divulging any secret if I say that this importance will surpass that of all three Pyramids, the site of the temple of Karnak, the Valley of the Kings, and the treasure of Tutankhamen as well, for the results will be a conclusive proof of the astonishing progress and matchless development achieved by the Ancient Egyptian civilization.

What is new is that the investigation will be essentially of a technological character; even so, its chief importance lies in its throwing luminous light on the personality of the ancient Egyptians. It will provide completely new material for sociologists, likewise for anthropologists. I would not be exaggerating if I said that this discovery would perhaps transcend in importance that of the atomic bomb or going into space.

What has prompted me to talk does not relate to what I previously mentioned. I do nevertheless want to say something about the actual operation of the investigation. How? And why? And who will undertake it? Without a precise and clearly defined answer to these questions, we would maybe fall into a fresh disaster, another national catastrophe to be added to the string of catastrophes with which we have been smitten throughout our national history. I would ask and hope that we do not carry out this examination now, despite what I said about its importance; I mean that we should not carry it out when we are in this state of deterioration in which we are living, eating our crust of bread for which we are indebted to others and making no reckoning now for our tomorrow. We are living according to the law of the jungle, where the large eats the small and the strong the weak. In short, this discovery would be a disaster, so long as our features remain so strangely distorted. Let us look at how we dress and how we eat and where we live and how we love and marry and bear children. We are completely encompassed by all the elements of deformity which have been imposed on us and to which we comply submissively day after day, without putting up any resistance, because the enemy comes to us each time with a thousand different faces and from a thousand different doors and windows. Why do we wear synthetic fibres in this suffocating weather when we grow cotton and flax? Why do we live in these gloomy buildings that resemble soap or shoe boxes, when we have in front of us the spacious desert? I shall not enumerate the tens of details of the deformities that dominate every single moment of our lives. But what I would say is that the unearthing of anything in the shrine of the Lady Atia would be a disaster when we are in our present state, for an operation of such significance and importance could not be accomplished without colossal effort and extraordinary material and human resources. Moreover, since the shrine lies in a very spacious area of land, this would entail the removal of the whole of the Greater Cemetery and the neighbouring districts.

The smacking of lips at the potentialities of this country

will increase in an unimaginable manner if the excavations take place now, especially as they will require the participation of foreigners in the research and investigative operations. I would not be exaggerating if I said that, because of them, there might well break out a new series of those classic imperialist wars familiar since the early years of the last century.

Finally, I would like to draw attention to the fact that the existence of the shrine of the Lady Atia in this place is no mere coincidence, for I am not a great believer in the law of coincidence. Everybody should thus try to search for the truth in this direction.

To Whom It May Concern

Despite the fact that the competent authorities, and the press, are keeping silent about the question of the shrine of the Lady Atia, by reason of numerous confusions that have not been precisely made known, and despite the magazine *al-Sabah* abandoning its decision to undergo an extensive investigation into the matter, yet, as the saying goes, the sword has forestalled his dismissal, for nothing is hidden that is not in time divulged and spread abroad. The question of the shrine of the Lady Atia has become the talk of people throughout the country; even a certain composer of low songs of the type that are all the rage these days, who likes to exploit opportunities, has written a song of this sort, the words of which go, 'O Atia, let us know how everyone is'. It can be easily listened to by taking one of the taxis plying between Cairo and the provinces.

As for the group of writers and journalists who make a living from writing in the petro-dollar papers and magazines, the question of the Lady Atia's shrine has been tantamount to a fortune falling on top of them from the heavens, especially because of the state of drought they were in owing to the absence of any exciting events within the countries they write about. And so they have taken to dealing with the question of the Lady Atia from every possible angle. The most amusing of them was a freelance journalist who is a specialist in writing for the papers and magazines of Arab organizations of diverse political trends. He first wrote trying to establish that the question of the shrine of the Lady Atia, during this period of time, has had as its primary aim the distracting of attention from the Iraq-Iran war. On the other hand, he wrote in a second magazine saying that the matter was a working touchstone around which the powers of resistance and opposition in the area must be rallied.

As for abroad, the correspondent of an English newspaper concerned with publishing news of underdeveloped countries presented a detailed report on the Lady Atia affair. In it he spurred his government, in an indirect way, to hurry up and lay hold of the matter before the governments of other foreign countries beat them to it, when they would only bite their fingers in regret. On the other hand, a well-known scandal magazine published indecent pictures of the delegate of an international cultural organization working in Cairo in sexual poses with the gravedigger of the shrine of the Lady Atia; under these pictures it contented itself with the caption: 'No comment'.

It is said that this delegate at once brought an action against the magazine demanding damages amounting to several million dollars.

However, what must be mentioned essentially is that everything we have set forth we would not have known about had it not been for the journalist Izzat Yousif who collected the basic material relating to the press investigation, material which has not been published. During that time she suddenly got married to the archaeologist Ali Faheem. After that she gave in her resignation irrevocably to the magazine, and a little later Ali Faheem passed away, having been run over by an unidentified car while on his way back home at night. At the time it was said that he had been complaining to his close friends of his continually having the sensation that he was being watched by persons unknown and that he had the feeling he was going to be killed.

Also, a short while before that the flat of the newlyweds had been the subject of a strange incident: unknown persons had raided the flat and destroyed its contents, after having searched through it. They had contented themselves with stealing certain papers belonging to the couple, and some books. When Ali Faheem informed the police, the inquiries revealed nothing and the incident was recorded as having been committed by some unknown person.

It seems that these two strange incidents made Izzat Yousif take things in hand in relation to a collection of facts which she and her husband knew about. For some reason they refrained from making these facts known, or perhaps they were prevented in some way or another from so doing. She apparently made a strange decision, before her mysterious disappearance from her house, according to what the papers later said.

The fact is that all we have recorded consists of no more than we found on a certain morning under the door of our flat in a medium-sized envelope. It contained what Izzat Yousif had written, neither more nor less, under the title 'To whom it may concern' and with her signature

appended but undated. Then, at the bottom of the page, 'Izzat Yousif may die, but the truth remains.'

The envelope of medium size that we found was the very same sort of envelope found by a number of persons under the doors of their homes. They all contained the same material and were entitled in each case 'To whom it may concern'.

DATE DUE - - - -

JUL 0 3 2000

BRODART, CO.   Cat. No. 23-221-003